LIMPY'S ADULT LEXICON

ALSO BY JOSEPH HEYWOOD

Woods Cop Mysteries
Ice Hunter (2001)
Blue Wolf in Green Fire (2002)
Chasing a Blond Moon (2003)
Running Dark (2005)
Strike Dog (2007)
Death Roe (2009)
Shadow of the Wolf Tree (2010)
Force of Blood (2011)
Killing a Cold One (2013)
Buckular Dystrophy (2016)
Bad Optics (2018)

Lute Bapcat Mysteries
Red Jacket (2012)
Mountains of the Misbegotten (2014)
Beyond Beyond (2020)

Other Fiction
Taxi Dancer (1985)
The Berkut (1987)
The Domino Conspiracy (1992)
The Snowfly (2000)

Short Story Collections
Hard Ground (2013)
Harder Ground (2015)
Upper Peculiar (2019)

Nonfiction-Memoir
Covered Waters: Tempests of a Nomadic Trouter (2003/2015)

Cartoons
The ABCs of Snowmobiling (1968)

LIMPY'S ADULT LEXICON

Raw, Politically Incorrect, Improper & Unexpurgated, As Overheard & Noodled By

JOSEPH HEYWOOD

Essex, Connecticut

An imprint of Globe Pequot, the trade division of
The Rowman & Littlefield Publishing Group, Inc.
4501 Forbes Blvd., Ste. 200
Lanham, MD 20706
www.rowman.com

Distributed by NATIONAL BOOK NETWORK

British Library Cataloguing in Publication Information Available

Library of Congress Cataloging-in-Publication Data

Names: Heywood, Joseph, author.
Title: Limpy's adult lexicon / raw, politically incorrect, improper &
 unexpurgated as overheard & noodled by Joseph Heywood.
Description: Essex, Connecticut : Lyons Press, [2023]
Identifiers: LCCN 2022051697 (print) | LCCN 2022051698 (ebook) | ISBN
 9781493072989 (cloth ; alk. paper) | ISBN 9781493072996 (epub)
Subjects: LCSH: Allerdyce, Limpy (Fictitious character) | Heywood,
 Joseph—Characters. | Heywood, Joseph—Literary style. | LCGFT: Literary
 criticism.
Classification: LCC PS3558.E92 Z68 2023 (print) | LCC PS3558.E92 (ebook)
 | DDC 813/.54—dc23/eng/20230309
LC record available at https://lccn.loc.gov/2022051697
LC ebook record available at https://lccn.loc.gov/2022051698

For

Mike and Monica Brown (& Zeta)
Ruth "Rootie" / "Mizz D" DiSilvestro
Dave & Diana Stimac (& Lucky)

TAPLE OF STUFF IN 'ERE

Part I

WORDS FROM THE WORD FIDDLER

What the heck is this little book about?

Well, it's about Limpy Allerdyce, and it's about words, and language . . . especially the creative misuse of both. And let me say right here at the starting line: I am *not* a lexicographer. I first landed on the shores of the Upper Peninsula in the summer of 1958, and have been collecting words and sayings ever since. When I began thinking about writing the Woods Cop mystery series more than two decades ago, I got really "serious" about gathering Yooper palaver.

Why focus on Limpy Allerdyce? He's not real, right?

In your mind, mebbe, but dat bugger talk me all time. Limpy dere is like da old wolfie oot dere on da Yooper taiga. Mebbe he lost da few teet', an' don't move so fast no more, but he can by sheer force of indomitable will, wisdom, and infamous reputation still compel a pack to follow his lead. I asked the old bird about this once, and here's what he had to say: "Da wolfie pack, dey don't stop follow 'cause main guy oldenin', wah!"

What I've collected is da mishymashy, which includes words Limpy uses with his odd pronunciations and definitions; words he's invented for his own use; words and pronunciations many Yoopers employ every day; smatterings of old trapper slang; and some bits and pieces of foreign languages that sometimes pop up in Yooper conversations, especially Finnish, Ojibwa, and French. Kind of a smorgasborg of lingo with a Limpy twist on most of it.

One little note: When Finns pronounce a "b," it often comes out as a "p," and sometimes she's da vicey versey, but not always, which I guess makes the whole thing rather quirky.

Certain critics and readers define writers as people who "fiddle with language." Scribblers such as the late mssrs. Shakespeare and Milton are prime examples, having created thousands of new words and phrases for their characters and their work during their legendary careers, with many many many of their words and sayings still in use today.

I once had a boss who referred to people he didn't agree with, or took exception to his views, as being "pieces of work." I doubt he knew the phrase was Shakespeare's. (I certainly didn't until much later.)

My Yooper friends sometimes ask, "Why da hell youse care about dis Shakespeare jamoke? He been down dere in da ground what, four hunnert year?"

Yep, he has surely been in deep-dirt-nap mode since 1616, so he's thoroughly, completely, entirely dead—yet his language is still quite alive! How much of our English will still be in use by the twenty-fifth century?

Scholars tell us that Shakespeare used 17,677 words in his 37 plays, 2 narrative poems, and 154 sonnets. Some scholars estimate he wholescale invented at least 1,700 of those words. In fairness, some of his pithier words and phrases may already have been in common use, and rather than him having invented them, he simply may have been the first writer to scribble them into his dramatic work and thereby create a record of them. The point here is that the man clearly was an imaginative artist with language, and words were his paint.

Yoopers are not so different. The fictional character Limpy Allerdyce is a little-tad-bit creative in how he employs vocabulary and language. Yet sometimes, while what he says may seem at first blush rather nonsensical, there is almost always a logic at work in what he says, and how he says it. I think he's rather an artist with language—in da man's own way, eh.

In this regard, Limpy is rather Shakespearean in that some words, terms, and phrases he employs are in common Yooper use, while others are strictly of his own invention. Limpy as Shakespearean? Such a thought makes me dizzy. (At my age, almost any thought makes me dizzy. Especially those involving good food, or brook trout fishing.)

Don't buy the Shakespeare stuff? Okay, have you ever heard Yoopers talk about "burning daylight"? It means "wasting time," which is a clever way to put it. This isn't a unique Yooper term. The phrase, with the same meaning, is in two of Shakespeare's plays, *Romeo and Juliet* and *The Merry Wives of Windsor.*

For the record: Shakespeare lived in the Elizabethan period, which lasted from Queen Elizabeth I's coronation in 1558 to her death in 1603. She became queen at age twenty-five, and died at seventy. Shakespeare outlived the old gal, and died in 1616 at age fifty-two.

Why all this stuff about Shakespeare?

Simple. Look around at private companies flying into space, smartphones and myriad apps, self-driving vehicles, social media, technological bells and whistles ad infinitum—all of this fast-moving, slick, marvelous, magical change. Even with all that has transformed so dramatically, the English language has not altered so very much.

While Elizabethans certainly pronounced words somewhat— or even drastically—differently than we do, we can at least in type and print make out what they were saying in their day, and if they didn't stroke out over our spectacular technology, they would no doubt be able to eventually make out our writing and speaking. Language is a constant that certainly changes, with new words coming into use every year, but unlike the guts of modern technology, whose intimacy and birth belong to a few specialists, language remains pretty much accessible to—and the property of—all of us. It is truly a universal treasure.

If we think we are standing on some majestic pinnacle, I think it's entertaining to remember that we are still, every day of our lives, using words and phrases that were in use four centuries ago, and no doubt some are even older than that. Examples just from Shakespeare include *have not slept one wink*; *the clothes make the man*; *in my heart of hearts*; *what's done is done*; *short shrift*; *tower of strength*; *melted into thin air*. Amazing, eh? You betcha!

And here are some of the words Shakespeare invented: *bandit*, *elbow* (as a verb), *skim-milk*, *unaware*, *lackluster*, *undress*, *uncomfortable*, *unreal*, *bloody*, *assassination*, *frugal*, *gnarled*, *laughable*, *suspicious*, *majestic*, and *lonely*. Totally *gnarly*, dudes! Who among us mighta-coulda-woulda thunk an all-purpose word such as gnarly from "surferdude-dom" quietly flowed down to us from Mr. Shakespeare (albeit, in another form, morphing from *gnarled* to *gnarly*). Holy wah!

I include this stuff only to remind us that language can be a road to other times and other places, and, if one listens carefully to how people speak, one's imagination may discover a lot of new and interesting flights of fancy.

Our lately departed Mr. Shakespeare aside, more recent authors like J. R. R. Tolkien went so far as to create entire new worlds, giving their new worlds their own languages (e.g., Quenya and Sindarin). (Tolkien's languages were based roughly on English, Welsh, and Finnish.)

In the United States we had Faulkner creating and/or embellishing regional Southern lingo for characters in his fictional Yoknapatawpha County in Mississippi.

James Joyce did similarly for both English and Irish, and multiple loaners (or word-bases) from too many other languages to count. Faulkner and Joyce, each in his own way, explored nonstandard grammar and syntax, and, in so doing, became master dialect "manipulators" (which is not a formal academic field of study).

The study of dialects began with the formation of the American Dialect Society in 1889, and one of the most important works in this field appeared in 1949: *A Word Geography of the Eastern United States*, compiled and written by University of Michigan professor Hans Kurath.

Author Bill Bryson, in *The Mother Tongue: English and How It Got That Way* (1990), wrote, "Whether you call a long cylindrical sandwich a hero (gyro), submarine, hoagy, torpedo, Garibaldi, poor boy, or any of a half-dozen other names tells us something about where you came from, and calling it cottage cheese, Dutch cheese, pot cheese, smear cheese, clabber or curd cheese tells us something more."

Bryson further points out, "Even within a single region, speech patterns blur into an infinitude of tiny variations." This observation holds true for the Upper Peninsula, which physically is the size of Vermont and New Hampshire glued together. ("Marquette County, in da Central Yoop, she bigger'n da hull demm state Rope Island," Limpy once told me. Who knew he was a student of geography.)

As Bryson implies, there are small dialect vocabulary differences in various parts of the U.P., and words and terms common in the western Yoop may not be so in the eastern U.P. Add to this the fact that some words common all across the Upper Peninsula may be pronounced or accented with slight differences, depending upon where one is. And to complicate matters further, we can pitch some occupational, ethnic, and local dialects into the regional stew.

The actual voices and dialects I heard most often growing up were semirural Upstate New Yorkian; deeply urban New York City Anglo-Irish (Dad's family); and very rural North Carolina–Mississippi S'uth'n (Mom's family). Growing up as a USAF brat in an integrated military, I was surrounded by dialects and accents from all over the country, which over time were softened or replaced by military militechnohomogololingo—a peculiar odd blend which sort of leveled out everyone's unique pronunciations or regional accents. As a kid, the ways people talked always captivated me, especially how they talked when they told stories.

Just as military-brat life more or less homogenized the brat pack, Yooper kids growing up and drooling over MTV shows began to lose some of their memorable Yooper patois and replaced it with the homogenized MTV global rock-your-cool-socks-off slango and such. Too early to tell how Facebook and other raging social networks are further eroding this, but the effect on how kids used to talk in the U.P. seems certain and clear. All you have to do is talk to kids up here to hear what's gone MIA (and unlikely to be retrieved or revived).

The first book that impressed me with language was Mark Twain's *Adventures of Huckleberry Finn*, where Huck told his tale from a young boy's viewpoint in what seemed to me—and I assume other readers, too—an authentic rural Southern dialect. When Twain's Black character Jim talked, Twain himself characterized Jim's lingo as "Missouri Negro dialect."

Twain's note notwithstanding, various scholars believe Twain drew from seven different dialects to reflect the speech patterns of various characters, and amazingly, all seven dialects came from the same small geographic area. Remember, Twain (Samuel Clemens) was born and grew up in Hannibal, MO, north of St. Louis, on the Mississippi River, which in his boyhood was a main jumping-off area for Americans seeking to go westward, and the main river highway north and south, so there were a lot of folks and different tongues hanging around, some who'd been there a while, and others just passing through. It's possible that there are even today thousands of tiny, localized, regional accents and dialects alive and well, many of them, if not most of them, unknown to scholars.

Let's throw in one final little nit at this point. The same word can have dramatically different meanings, depending on where you are in the world. For example, if you are in southeast England, that blizzard threatening your life and limb would likely be viewed by

Upper Peninsula residents as mere flurries or snow "spits." Location-location-location, and the rule of relativity—not Einstein's gobbledygook, but rather the notion that in practice, the theory is different. Wah.

What I learned in all of my own wide-flung reading and life experiences has been that you don't have to hold a PhD or be extensively and formally educated with multiple degrees to be able to effectively communicate feelings and thoughts. There are some damn smart people in this world who have had very limited formal educations, but their brains are often second to none.

Never mind Mark Twain. More recently, we had the late Larry McMurtry's whole series of characters in *Lonesome Dove* (and in its prequels, corollaries, and spin-offs). McMurtry created a Texas accent through nonstandard spelling and regional slang which rang true to me, especially since there was a time when the Air Force Heywoods lived in Texas (and Oklahoma), a time in which I found both states to be quasi-foreign countries—not unlike our family's several years in *Firenze e Napoli, Italia*.

I never found dialects and linguistic shenanigans off-putting in the stories I was reading, or heard. Dialects made stories seem to me to be *more authentic*, and thus more compelling. Most of all they seemed to make certain languages in certain circumstances almost musical in their cadence, and I liked this effect a lot. I was always spellbound, listening to my Ma—my grandmother, Mary Heywood, and her sisters, Aunt Alice, Aunt Bea, Aunt Betty, and Aunt Kitty—go at it when they got together. (All of them were "off the boat" from Castleblayney, Ireland, County Monaghan, north of Dublin, along the Northern Ireland border.) I can still hear them jabberjabbing and yipyapping at each other when I close my eyes.)

Flash forward many decades and into my mind crawled a character who called himself Limpy Allerdyce, who was, as I was to learn, a master poacher-predator-violator, who, for his most lucrative and legally risky jobs, works alone, and keeps his mouth shut. In my twenty years of riding along with Michigan conservation officers during their daily routine (and various special-purpose) patrols, I have learned that the best, most successful poachers keep to themselves, and keep very quiet. Just like illegal wolf-whackers now afoot in the U.P. whose motto is "Shoot, shovel, and shut up."

Many local violators are much gossiped about in their rural communities, and, like most gossip, there can be seeds and kernels of truth embedded in shovels-full of manure (talk about Fake News). You might be surprised at the way successful COs carefully and painstakingly sift through rumors for hints and tips about violators' habits and activities. Such things can provide valuable leads in making certain cases. Just as investigative reporters learn to never dismiss a possible story kernel out of hand, so too it is for conservation officers, who must carefully consider and weigh everything they hear. The best officers are exquisite listeners who have developed a skill for picking up on exactly what is said—how it is said, when it is said—and at the same time, they also learn to recognize what's *not* being said, which is sometimes far more important than the actual information.

The most successful poacher-violators rarely get pinched—unless a particular officer decides that he or she will make a concerted effort to analyze and understand a particular suspect by studying how the individual works. In such instances, and over time, a CO can assemble, through careful investigation and study, enough essential intel and evidence to organize warrants and an effective arrest (and, more importantly, to sustain a successful prosecution).

Some violators are violent psychopaths. Over the years many of Michigan's wildlife law enforcement officers have died, a sick testament to the sad fact of high risk in this line of work.

Other violators may be rough-hewn, but are not inherently violent. This type of violator sometimes comes to relish the psychological cat-and-mouse games played against conservation officers, and against their own competitors, and sometimes this sort enjoys the game-playing more than the fruits of actual poaching. And yes, some of these violators are highly competitive, and yes, they even have in their minds a sort of hierarchy of rankings for local ne'er-do-wells, with their own rank clearly at or near the top of such imaginary ratings ladders.

Another strange and interesting phenomenon I've encountered during my many years in trucks is that some old poachers eventually lose their relish for "mind games" with game wardens, and when they finally have to face one who's as secretive, sneaky, determined, stubborn, and mentally tough as themselves, they sometimes flip-flop from violating to snitching.

They do this for a number of reasons. To make their own lives easier. Or to make the lives of their competitors on that comparative ladder much more difficult, or—and this is rare—because they suddenly see the stark reality of what they have wrought on local wildlife and resources over their many decades of violating. There's a lot of twisted logic in such thinking, but the bad-boy-turns-snitch phenomenon is quite real.

Over my lifetime I've lived in Chippewa, Luce, Schoolcraft, Delta, Marquette, Baraga, Menominee, and Keweenaw Counties for varying amounts of time. In my almost twenty years of working with Michigan conservation officers, I've patrolled all fifteen U.P. counties, plus more than forty counties BTB (Below the Bridge). I have witnessed firsthand the old-poacher-as-snitch, and in a couple of cases, the poachers also opened up to me, which proved invaluable both to me *and* to my partners. I also learned that some of these violators had read my books, and were even fans; in such moments I was relieved that early on in the series I had decided not to reveal our Michigan conservation officers' full playbook of operational techniques and methods. And I still don't.

I would hastily and regrettably add here that we encountered at least as many violators who were entirely illiterate as those capable of reading any books. This was a sad, embarrassing moment for all involved, and a real eye-opener for me. So many people who can't read a lick, in this country? Scary, and truly sad.

When readers first encounter Allerdyce, it is in the first Woods Cop book, called *Ice Hunter*. Grady Service has just come from a court appearance and is met by his sergeant. Their exchange goes like this:

> "Grady . . . Allerdyce is getting an early release."
>
> Service stared at her. Limpy Allerdyce had spent the last seven years in Jackson at the State Prison of Southern Michigan, a maximum-security, walled prison built a long time ago.★ Allerdyce was one of the most notorious poachers in state history, and Service had put him away for attempted murder. Allerdyce was the leader of a tribe of poachers, mostly his relations, who lived like animals in the far southwestern reaches of Marquette County. They killed bears and sold gall bladders and footpads to Korean brokers in Los Angeles for shipment to Korea and Taiwan. They killed dozens of deer, took thousands of fish, and got substantial money for their take from buyers in Chicago and Detroit. Despite their income, the clan lived like savages. Service had not expected Allerdyce to be turned loose for several more years.

Limpy was sentenced and sent BTB to Jackson for attempted murder, but like many people incarcerated for serious crimes, overcrowding and good behavior got him an early release. Doesn't seem right, but that's reality in our prison system.

Thomas Wolfe once called someone who lived in a certain way in a certain isolated part of the country an "unspeakable lying homunculus, bubble-headed rat." He wasn't speaking of Allerdyce, of course, but Wolfe's words made me think immediately of Limpy.

Over time, some readers may begin to suspect more depth to this odd character, and that perhaps he's not quite what his public exposure first suggests. I describe him in *Ice Hunter*: Like Shakespeare's

---

★SPSM is but one of the prison's names from the time of the incident described. It was also called Southern Michigan Prison, Jackson State Prison, Jackson Prison, Jacktown, and several others. The institution was built in 1839, the first prison in Michigan, and is still in use today. My word choice for the prison and other institutions and formal titles is admittedly arbitrary, the sort of choices we all make every day in talking to each other. Most of the time such choices are not monumental in damaging what it is we are trying to pass on.

outrageous character Falstaff, Allerdyce exhibits little doubt in himself, and though he seems to have a dark view of life, and living, there are glimpses of other lights at other levels sometimes flashing like distant small beacons or markers. Unlike Falstaff, who virtually everyone is happy to see and be around (until they aren't), no one is *ever* glad to see Limpy. His reputation scares the hell out of everybody he comes in contact with, and most who've only heard about him—everyone but Grady Service, whose late father (also a CO) had jousted with, and bested, him.

Eventually we begin to see Allerdyce through new eyes, as he changes over several installments of the Woods Cop series. It may be more accurate to say the old violator *seems* to be changing, because our protagonist Grady Service is never entirely certain. Neither am I, nor are the readers—not even the most rabid, diehard Limpy-loving fans. Because of the character's reputation, and also based on what we have seen of his actual behaviors, we are all compelled to keep our eyes on the man. Has he changed? Well, it appears so—at times. But the series hasn't finished yet, and I guess we shall see what we shall see.

When I created Limpy (more accurately, when Allerdyce mostly created himself), I did not expect him to become a favorite of many readers, but he quickly did, and remains so. Many fans seem fascinated by him in ways that elude me. The man certainly has a singular, yet not fully explicated, personality, and he has a history with Grady Service's father. From this he's developed an apparently very real affection for the conservation officer son, despite once accidentally shooting Grady during a scuffle while being arrested, and for that, doing hard time in the State Prison of Southern Michigan in Jackson (aka, Jacktown, or SPSM). Hell, even *I* don't trust him.

Limpy's character speaks the lingo of an old-time Yooper, a form of bent bush-Canuck. As a language-fiddler, I knew early on that using Yooperese put me on the precipice of a potential minefield. Dialects are not uniformly popular with editors, readers, or critics, yet when they work, they can add some real muscle to the fictional world the writer is trying to shape and describe.

I make no pretense of trying to create a full-blown language; rather, I "borrow" from Yooper slang, some of it modern, and some of it a bit more dated, the kind of things that a man of Limpy's years might likely acquire and employ across his life. His manner of speech, then, is a "sludgegullion" of standard English, rural Yooper slang, and some Trumpian locker-room talk. There are many malapropisms, the logic for which sometimes makes damn good, if twisted, sense.

I once had a friend who constantly said "normanclature" for "nomenclature," and "condomominium" for "condom." He had a college degree—not in the literary arts—and was astonishingly creative and plenty smart. But he was also imprinted with the lingo he heard growing up in East Texas. (His grandma took a ride in her house most of the length of Galveston Island during a monster hurricane in a previous century.) Like my friend, all of us are imprinted to various degrees by where we grow up, and how our families, friends, and others in our communities talk and think. Such influence is unavoidable, and becomes part of who we are.

A report I once read characterized Yooper language as Inland Northern American English (or Great Lakes Dialect). Limpy's Yooperese is, of course, based on a mixture of Yooper mixalated lingos, but it is primarily Canadian, not Yooper Finnglish—as some seem to think. Many folks also wrongly believe that Finns were the most numerous foreign immigrants into Michigan, but they were not. *Canadians* were (duh: location-location-location!), while Finns were among the smaller immigrant groups to the U.P. Nonetheless, Finnish people are now either the largest, or nearly the largest, ethnic group in the area, with the most recent figure (from the year 2000) at 16 percent. The Finns, you might say, have had a much larger impact on Yooper culture than their size might suggest (which has been true of the country of Finland, too).

Have all readers enjoyed my use of dialect and odd vocabulary? Newp, clearly not. One fan wrote to chew me up and down over my use of Yooper slang, accusing me of making up "the whole damn thing." I told him to go to Tina's Catalina, a café in South Range, just over the hill south of Houghton, and have breakfast or lunch or a delicious hunk of fresh "bakery," sit back, and just listen to the cross-table talk, and the interactions with the waitresses. I guaranteed him he would hear the lingo pretty close to the way Allerdyce spits it out. Don't believe me? Go see for yourself.

I once had an older woman sharply but civilly call me out for denigrating Yoopers because I had dared to write that there were bullet holes in all the road signs above the bridge. She was indignant, insisting there were no such holes in the signs where *she* lived. I still don't know where that is, but I've been all over the U.P., and it is rare to find any signs absent bullet holes or shotgun pellet perforations. The detail about the signs was meant to provide local color, not to insult people, but one learns early on as a writer that everything you write will insult or anger someone. Frankly, after a while, one doesn't even see the bullet holes anymore. There's a church in Grand Marais with a bullet hole in one of its stained-glass windows, and I doubt many parishioners have ever even noticed it. (I once used this fact in a short story.)

With this lexicon, I hope you get a better feel for Mr. Allerdyce's mind and unique view of the world. His outlook is admittedly raw, and my presentation, unexpurgated. Let me assure you, dear reader, that not everyone in the U.P. is like Allerdyce, in accent or attitude. Most people up here are law-abiding, good citizens, and damn good neighbors.

Just recently I was walking on a county road with my notebook and when a small white pickup truck went by, it quickly spun around, came back past me, made another fast 180, and came back yet *again*, this time pulling up beside me and stopping.

The driver rolled down the window and said, "Are you okay? Do you need help?"

"No help needed, I'm good," I told him. "Just out walking and looking around. Thanks for asking."

I had a notebook in one hand and a ballpoint pen in the other. My wife Jambe Longue was just up the road with our dog Shaksper, and both of them fell back, laughing their butts off.

You see, there is (or was) a group home for dementia patients somewhere nearby, and I assume that residents from there had a habit of going for unscheduled walkabouts. This sort of thing—being intercepted as an addlepated old codgertarian wanderer—really shores up the old self-image . . . but oh God, what a wonderful life moment, *and* story. It made my day.

Who wants to read about folks who follow all the rules? I mean, do you want to read about sinners, or saints?

I hope you have as much fun with this language as I've had. I've been collecting this vocabulary and these expressions roughly since 1958. Friends up in Pine Stump Junction (ten miles south of the Lake Superior shoreline) have told me that in the long winters between Woods Cop books, whilst playing Eight Ball at the bar or at my friend's place in Deer Park, and whilst imbibing copious quantities of beer, they would frequently "entertain" each other with Limpyisms— some from my books, and some which they invented on the spot, *en plein bière*. (As an author, I *loved* hearing this.)

Now for some technical notes regarding pronunciation.

There are in the world of dictionaries and pronunciations an estimated thirty-one possible specific ways within five categories (methods) to help us pronounce words. The five methods are as follows:

1. First syllable accented with secondary stress on penultimate (next to the last syllable);

2. First syllable accented with secondary stress on antepenultimate (third syllable of a word, counting backward from the last one);

3. First syllable accented without secondary stress;

4. First syllable accented in three-syllable versions; and

5. Second syllable accented.

Which approach or approaches shall we use?

Who cares.

This book came about because I just listened to Limpy (who talks to me a lot) and wrote down it da best way I could what I heard da man say. This is Limpy's Language, not some attempt to create a formal and intimidating, dipped-in-literary-history, Oxy-ooperford Dictionary. This small book is laid out more or less alphabetically, which seems to me the most straightforward approach. The word as I understood it appears in one typeface, with Limpy's version in a slightly different typeface. That's it—the totality of technical notations.

Enough wit' da jaw-jaw, an' da yak-yak. Dig in and enjoy. Feel free to make up new Limpyisms and have fun with this.

And thanks for supporting our Michigan conservation officers. They guard our wonderful state's vast natural resources so that our children and our grandkittles will be able to enjoy them like we and those before us have.

I finished the initial draft of this work back on St. Valentine's Day. How appropriate to complete a work of love about a subject, place, and people I love and respect on such a day.

—Joseph Heywood
Kells, Michigan (a semiquasidistant suburb
of Stephenson, Mid-Menominee County)
September 1, 2022

Part II

LIMPY'S THIRTY RULES FOR WANNABE VIOLATORS

RULE 1: "Dere ain't no rules."

RULE 2: "Work alone."

RULE 3: "Keep youse's yap shut."

RULE 4: "Dere a lot, take a lot. Dere jus' some small tad bit, take it all."

RULE 5: "Da game wardens can come ooten nowhere, so keep youse's head in game all da time."

RULE 6: "Da good game wardens always work, no matter da weather, or da time or da day. Youse got one of dese guys, gals near youse, go violate somewheres else."

RULE 7: "Don't use no stuff youse can't 'ford lose. (Dis include da truck youse drivin'.)"

RULE 8: "Youse happen pop-drop a wolfie, 'member da t'ree esses: Shoot, shovel, an' shut up."

RULE 9: "One shot's best when youse see youse's target, or shootin' from truck wit' da spotlight at night."

RULE 10: "Always carry DNR hunt-fish license an' game tag, jus' in case game warden shows up. Youse don't got tags an' license, youse got trouble. Don't give 'em no easy pinch."

RULE 11: "If youse is jacklightin', shoot da deer, but come back later ta find it, gut it, an' get it ooten dere."

RULE 12: "Come July, if it red, it dead. Da meat's a lot tastier in July den late fall or winter."

RULE 13: "Dere's like two hunnert game wardens an' dey all talkin' each udder. Youse pick fight wit' one, youse gone have ta fight da hull demm two hunnert. Dey stick togedder, eh?"

RULE 14: "Always know when da game warden is in 'is house. Youse got pay somebody watch 'is house an' 'is truck, an' call youse, den do 'er. Dis hull lot cheaper den DNR fines, 'specially dese days."

RULE 15: "Some jamoke come up to youse at bar from Shitcongo or da Motown, an' ask youse get da sport a deer or bear wit'out 'im 'avin' no license, don't take dat job till youse got da sport's cash in da hand, an' da sport, 'e knows even den, dere ain't no guarantee."

RULE 16: "Best time, place ta shoot timberdoodles [American woodcock] is when she just startin' get dark on da two-tracks, an' youse can see youse's muzzle flash."

RULE 17: "If womyn gots gun in hand an' wants talk, youse best stop an' listen."

RULE 18: "If dat sneaky game warden sidle up ta youse all of sudden an' acts real chummy, an' asks, 'Youse drinkin'?', don't youse answer, 'Why, youse buyin'?"

RULE 19: "Youse never tell nobody where youse catched da big specs [brook trout], not even da wifey nor da squeeze when dey gettin' frisky on da whiskey."

RULE 20: "Da game wardens 'speck youse ta lie, so tell dem da trut' an' mess wit' dere minds."

RULE 21: "Never take same or da direct way inta or outta da huntin' or fishin' spot."

RULE 22: "When game warden asks youse if youse understan' youse's rights, tell him youse didn't hear nuttin' after 'Youse got right remain silent.' Get a lawyer right den."

RULE 23: "Good violator know how ta punt, eh? Bug out before dey take youse out."

RULE 24: "When youse get caught wit' da red hands (an' youse will), don't run. Most dose game wardens are younger, in better shape, an' better at fightin' den youse. Even da old ones not in shape know all da dirty fight tricks."

RULE 25: "Don't never piss off da womyn (or wymyns) in youse's life. Da game wardens make more busts from pissed-off wives an' girlfriends den anyt'ing else."

RULE 26: "If you know where dere's lots of game or fish, you can bet game wardens know dis too."

RULE 27: "Will come day when game warden will pinch youse, an' write youse da tickets. Don't get pissed, an' don't be growin' no chip on youse's shoulder. Tickets is jus' cost of do' bidnet oot in woods."

RULE 28: "Youse huntin' from tree stand, an' game warden walkin' toward youse, don't be pointin' rifle or slug-gun 'is or 'er way. Dat *really* piss dem off."

RULE 29: "Youse end up before da jutch, don't be in dere wit'out no lawyer."

RULE 30: "If youse keep gettin' pinched, find somepin' else ta do. Dey pinch youse too many times, dey call you habitual bad boy or girlie, an' stick you not in da county lockup, but in da state prison wit' big bad jamokes got names like Icepick an' Toe Tag."

Part III

ALLERDYCEAN WISDOM & WIT (UNEXPURGATED & NOT CENSORED NEITHER)

On opponents of good forest management: "Youse hate logging? Try wipin' wit da plastic."

On seein' an attractive young woman: "She da unmilked cow, dat one."

On golf: "Gott invent golf, keep jamokes an' assholes offen trout streams."

On pasty-eating etiquette: "Dere's screws loosed in pipples wants use da ketchups an' da cravy on dere pasties."

On something really difficult to do: "Dat like try put nips on bobcat."

On being unsuited or unqualified: "Like brogan on duck's foot."

On very, very long odds: "T'ird down an' len'th a da Mississippi ta go."

On something difficult to see: "Like watchin' eels in washmachine."

On being slow-footed: "Too slow ta even carry da cold soup."

On appearances: "Like da stone boat. Can look real good, but she won't float, eh?"

On hard work without result: "Wet ass an' da empty net."

On difficult circumstances: "Cold as takin' crap in steel port-da-john in Jan'wary whiteout."

On obfuscating facts when somebody asks, "Catch anything today?": "Nuttin' over six pounds." (Dis no lie. True fact: Even zero fish ain't over six pounds.)

On untrustworthiness: "Crooked as a dog's hind leg."

On subtlety: "Uncle Amo, 'is edacations got da interrupt when he got drafted. Too demm bad, dat: 'e was almost done seven crade."

On curiosity: "Eino, one day tooken 'is nose apart ta see how she run."

On rank stupid: "Dere's dat Finnlander tooken TP to da crap game."

On accidental deaths: "Toivo's brudder, Beek Onte, gotten kilt while drinkin' da white milks. Wah, da cow she fallened over on 'im!"

On cultural logic: "Can allas tell if Finnlander on da level. Got da snoose runnin' ooten bot' side of 'is mout'."

On denizens of gated communities: "Snow Whites an' Ivory Snowmans onny."

On people who lack substance or gravitas: "Dat jamoke all laces, no boots."

On the female perception of suspicious cultural male values: "How come oot camp youse call me sweetheart, in town youse call me hello?"

On relative size: "Big as da Marquette County, which dat bigger'n hull state dey call Rope Island. Da Yoop, she bigger den Mary's Land, an' Vertmont–New Hamshares Gorilla-stucken togedder."

On multiple difficult tasks: "Like sortin' cats afore youse try 'erd 'em."

On Internet dating: "It jus' some kinda get-some-on-da-outside-game."

On a hopelessly inept person: "Jamoke goin' nowheres wit' nuttin' an' comin' back wit' less."

On being doomed: "Got less chance den skeetie in bat's night beam."

On the value of truth: "First lie win if she come before da trut'."

More on truth: "Da bigger da lie, da more pipples buy it, an' dere ain't no lie can't be amped a hull lot bigger."

On bad visibility: "Dis fog t'icker'n gray Jell-O."

On name-calling: "Sticks an' stones won't break no bones, lessen youse put 'em in wool nips an' swing it like a cop's sap: den dem bones'll break, you betcha."

On being out of place: "Welcome as Mooslum at da midnight mass, eh."

On U.P. road quality: "Dere's real bad, bad, bad roads—an' den dere's Luke's Road up Nort' Iron County, an' she's da worst uvda worst."

On time passing slowly: "Dat clock movin' like woolly worm inside da snowbank."

On politics: "Jamoke aks youse what youse t'ink LSD? Tell 'im youse didn't vote for da guy."

On befuddlement: "Glassy-eyed as dead pig wit' apple in 'is mout'."

On bad nerves: "He was tight as pine snake too long oot in da sun."

On the effect of male libido: "Sometimes get horny as pine snake in June, or big buck in da rut sees ten doe an' can't make up bloody mind, so he just stand dere an' spin like top."

On marksmanship: "He shoot so good he can pick one skeetie outen t'ousand and drill 'im twixt the eyes."

On defining slippery: "Dis ice slicker'n rock snot."

On winter effects: "Da winter ground frost 'ere, she reachin' down almost China, eh?"

On bad driving: "Jamoke so bad demoliton derby tell 'im get lost!

On people from Illinois: "Da FIBTABs come up 'ere from Shit-congo, stealin' our fish, takin' da wild-ass shots at sounds only mutts can 'ear."

On hunter safety: "Wunt trust some dose jamokes wit' da Ping-Pong ball gun."

On a terrible cook: "She da chef of da flash-fry-no-taste meat, wit' 'er bad breat' da onny spice give anyt'ing flavor. Uncook catcher's mitt got more flavor den anyt'ing she cookin' up."

On fudging age: "Dat old girlie been twenty-nine mebbe twenty-nine times."

On approximating weight: "She don't weigh but ounce or two over half-quarter ton."

On inhaling meals: "Some loggers eat dere lunch faster'n can say word."

On winter safety: "Don't eat none dat dere yellow snow."

On hunting and fishing: "First ice, best ice, and last ice, best ice, an' in between, youse's guess good as mine."

On announcing danger and an emergency: "O Cheesus! Da bear's loose!"

On asking for something: "Borrow me a beer an' a smoke, eh?"

On black people in Da Yoop, Limpy to Luticious Treebone, retired Detroit Metro cop:

> Limpy: "Can count number youse's pipples up 'ere above Da Britch on two hands."
>
> Treebone: "You're holding up one hand, you old fool."
>
> Allerdyce: "See, told youse."

On poor prospects: "'Boot as good as anteater huntin' in da snowbanks."

On unnecessary: "Useless as pockets on kittly cat."

On extreme smells: "Da dead moose in summer smell like da runny dinosaur crap."

On things putrid: "Worser'n ferret piss in noon sun."

On sobering up fast: "Racin' like hell-bat toorts home from da tavern-crawl tour at Oh-dark turdy, ain't nuttin' sober youse up quicker'n find cut-off pipple-head layin' on da snowmobile trail."

On weather: "Mother Nature, she callin' all da shots."

On finding Lansing from da U.P.: "Go east or west till smell it, den crosst-over Da Britch, den go sout' till youse step in it."

Defining Mission Impossible: "Making whoopie standin' up onda hammock inda windstorm."

Defining unsatisfying: "Like dry-humpin' on back of Skidoo wearin' armor suit, an' new Sorels."

On mixing up language: "I did already my walk."

On a foregone conclusion: "Pennies to pasties." (This would sound like *Bennies ta basties*.)

On more sentence twisting: "Put down on da bar da beer."

On in practice, lingo theory is different: "T'row da deer over da fence some bait."

More on lingo theory: "Somepin's out dere today gettin' me."

On verbal foreplay: "Pull offen not youse's clothes till we in da truck, eh."

On hearing worthless advice: "Take wit' grain uvda saltines."

On an unexpected bonus: "Dat's jus' icin's on da lake."

On want vs. need: "Youse may want two assholes, but youse onny need da one youse got."

On reality: "Huntin' ain't no game for da game."

On addiction: "Guy stuck on da drugs is like wood tick stuck on bear dog's ass."

On b.s. and the supernatural, etc.: "UFOs is like dose goofy air castles pipples dreams up. Dere ain't none 'cept in dere minds. Onny times I seen UFOs was in bar fights, and dose was real, an' flyin' at me!"

On the ultra environmentally sound, green burial: "I got in my last willin' sendiment dat I want da Yooper Hambone Dead-Guy Rite. Dis how she work: Youse go down to Red Owl, buy

$2.99 hambone, ram dat bone uppen my dead ass, an' drop me oot in da woods for da wolfies an' other predeaters."

On saying nothing whilst trying to say something (or perhaps saying something one doesn't mean to communicate?): "I forgot to remember."

On Yooper quickity thinking: Yooper in bar says, "Onny t'ing we ever get down from da Canucks is 'ockey players and hoors!" Canadian jumps up, yells, "My wifey's from Canada, eh!" Da quickt'inkin' Yooper smiles, says, "So what position da wifey she play?"

On introverts and extroverts: "Youse allas know when youse meet extrovert Finnlander: He be starin' at youse's feets, an' not 'is own."

On Finnish cultural values: "How dose Finnlanders dey celebrate da huge life t'ing? Dey don't tell nobody. Dey go home an' sit alone in da dark drinkin' da vodka, t'inkin' aboot herrings."

On wifely to husbandly communication: "Dere was dis Finnlander was techie an' da gamer, an all dat weird stuff. Wifey one day, she say, 'Sammi, love, youse run over ta da Red Owl, get gallon of milk, an' if dey gotten da fresh eggs, get six.' Sammi soon comes back wit' six gallons uvda milk an' wifey looks at all it, ask, 'What da heck all dis?' Sammi says, 'Dey had da fresh eggs, eh?'"

On expressing spousely affection: "Eino, he love 'is wife Liisa so much 'e pert-near tole her . . . once."

The difference between a Russian wedding and a Finnish funeral: "Dere one less drunk at Finnish funeral."

On questionable conversational skill: Toivo greets distant relative with question, "How many youse's uncles commit da suicides so far dis year?"

On Fake News with a Finnish twist: "The newspapers said how da Donald t'ought Finland belong Russia. When Finnish foreign minister he asked about dis, he said, "Yah, sure. We t'ought same t'ing aboot Trump.""

On knowing what one doesn't know: "Eino an' chum Alpo from Michigammee, go Marquette, walk down Washington Street, run inta priest dey know fum over Champion-way. Da guy's arm is in a cast. Alpo says to priest, 'Hey dere, Fadder, what happen ta youse's arm?' Da priest says, 'Oh, I slippin' in da bath-tub and broke 'er, eh.' After da priest walked on, Alpo asks Eino, 'What's bat-tub?' Eino shrugs, den in da shoulder t'umps Alpo reel hard: 'How I'm s'pose ta know, I ain't Cat-lick.'"

On da U.P. generally: "She's da simple, complexicated place, eh. Luffer or leafer."

On Limpy's "chum," Grady "Sonnyboy" Service: "Long time back me an' Sonnyboy had us nasty scrap an' I shotten 'im on ac-cident and dere 'e was, bullet in da leg, 'im bleedin' all over, and 'e given *me* da first ache! 'Is old man was great, tough game war-den. Sonnyboy way better, and not no drunk like 'is old man was. Sonnyboy got what da Finnlanders call da *sisu*. He get after you, he don't *never* quit. Sonnyboy don't t'ink like mos' game wardens. Sonnyboy allas t'inkin' outside da fox, like time he took da train injun crosst stretch weren't no udder way get to. Or time he para-chute into da Garden, alone, at night, in white dirt storm. When come ta violators, Sonnyboy GIVE IT, alla time, no quarter. Like 'is gold batch is way of life, not just job. He don't live like normal pipples, and 'e my chum."

Part IV

LIMPYSPEAK/YOOPERSPEAK (SPOKENABULARY)

NOTES TA YOUSE 'BOOT TA READ DIS STUFF:

1. Limpy Allerdyce's pronunciation and/or his peculiar word for something may or may not be U.P.-wide.

2. Finnish influences often cause the letter "b" to be pronounced as the letter "p." Likewise, for reasons unknown, "c" and "g" sometimes get mixed up and swapped.

3. Often older Yoop speakers don't distinguish singular from plural.

4. There is also a tendency to leave out prepositions and often conjunctions as well.

5. The difference between Yooper talk and rural talk in other parts of the country is one of speed. Yoopers can talk *very* fast, even when not excited. It is similar to the differences between speaking Canadian (Québécois) French vs. Parisian French, or regular English vs. New Yawklish.

A

aboot = about

accidentic = academic

acker = actor; also, "faker"

acquaintenance = acquaintance; also "squaintance"

across't = across; "on da udder side, eh"

Adam & Steve = da first gay guys, eh

adder = hatter; "Like dat creepo jamoke in dat Alice Vanderland place made da hats an' gotta made postal by da stuff?"

ad hunk = ad hoc

adminosphere = somewhere without action or oxygen

Adolph's Meat Tenderizer = Prime ingredient in do-it-yourself anti–bug itch therapy. Pour some powder in palm of your hand, add a little water to make a thick paste, then pile it on the bite site. Especially effective against blackflies. Yes, it will come off in bed at night, but better a little sand in your sheets than bloody from madly scratching yourself all night. Blackflies used to be "done" by early July. But nowadays, it seems, they go through several hatches and often are still lingering in the autumn, though the fall venom seems a bit less than midsummer. Blackflies hatch in clear, cold running water (trout water), unlike mosquitoes, which hatch in stagnant still waters.

aff = half

Affected Time Disorder (ATD) = Disorientation brought on by split time zones, with U.P.–Wisconsin border counties on Central time and all the rest on Eastern time. ATD is not to be confused with

SAD, Seasonal Affective Disorder, a kind of distraction-depression caused by gray skies and endless winters. FYI, average snowfalls in many areas are more than two hundred inches and snows come seven months a year.

AFLANK! = "Da TV ads' Duckgab" (Aflac)

agate launch = avalanche

age of consent = "When dey can reach over da bar for dere beers, eh?"

Ah-hi-yah = Ohio

aina = [Finnish] always

airbomb = really loud sudden noise

airgobang = "Tire airgobang [blowout] can make an airbomb when she goes, eh?"

airhankie = Nose-clearing-technique (sometimes called "The Farmer"); not considered polite in urban or suburban locales (meaning, when others may be looking).

airline = Trapper term for the straightest line between two points. [Author's note: In more modern bush talk, the term is "crow-fly," and both terms mean proceeding directly from A to B with no intermediate stops.]

air pudding = Finnish dish; uncooked farina, sugar, lemon juice. Can use cranberry sauce as well.

air rat = flying squirrel

Alberta clipper = Winter storm that sweeps down the plains of Canada, gathers snow crossing Lake Superior, and dumps it on the U.P.

alchologus = catchy, infectious, addictive

alefin = alevin; a young fish still in egg sac

alevipe = alewife; "'Member dose icky-bitty fish da salmons eat? Good t'ing too. 'Member when dose t'ings used die by t'ousands, washed up onna beaches, nasty stink so bad people no more allatime go beach. Have use dozers gettin' dem offen da beaches. Not no problem so much no more since da DNR made da salmon plants."

allatime = all the time

allda = all of the

alldasun, allsun = all of a sudden; suddenly, without warning

alleyball = basketball played on streets, highways, and in alleys in Yooper villages

all indents and porpoises = all intents and purposes

Alpo & Gravy Train = Horses in Limpy's dark humor; a hint at their futures?

aluminimity = anonymity

aluminum hatch = Term for summer season when rivers and cricks are overrun by canoes, kayaks, and tubing flotillas, forcing trout fishermen to seek beachhead seats until the drunken show passes in review, a sort of informal Macy's Thanksgiving Day parade, with the turkeys doing the floating. Some entomologically twisted sorts call it the "Hatch of Aluminus Flotillas."

Amasa = (pronounced *AM-uh-suh*) A former logging town nort' a (of) Crystal Falls, in da Iron County.

ambaguous = ambiguous

ambuglance = ambulance; emergency services veek; "Dey allas make youse look, eh, all dat racket dey go by"; also, "whambulance" amfibiatin = amphibian; "Like da frock [frog], hey?"

Amina = Limpian contraction, shortening of "I'm going to . . ."

ampitexturist = ambidexterous, or bot'-'anded

AMTRANKs = "Trains just for dose pipples go stooped over ride da rails."

anadromous = Fish who make spawning runs up rivers, and afterward return to larger bodies of water.

Anatomy Awards = Academy Awards

angel = angle

angel slobber = dat whitey meringue stuff dey use in some pies

anger wymyns = TV anchorwomen

angle = angel

Anteeksi = [Finnish] "Sorry."

anthinkstun = attention

antsindapantsy = antsy

apocketfullalips = apocalypse; "Youse know, when youse got too many of da womyn friends."

appalos = Trapper version of shish kebab: lean meat and fat, alternated with veggies, all skewered on a sharp stick and roasted over a low fire.

appetiddy = appetite

Appies = Apostolic Lutherans

applecard = applecart

Apple Knocker = Anyone hailing from Down Below (L.P. = Lower Peninsula, or BTB = Below the Bridge). Stems from insistence on using apples to bait deer, something old-timer Yooper hunters would never condescend to.

Area, da = "Where youse is now, like dis spot, or some place oot inda woods, in town, coundity [county], steak [state], Earfth [Earth], like dat."

ark = art

Ark on da Rocks = summer art show in Marquette, Michigan

army ant = drone, groupie, follower; not an individual

aroun' = around

arrow roads = one-way streets

artyfacial inspermination = artificial insemination

Arvon, Mount = "Da highest place in state. She just east of L'Anse [Baraga County] in the Urine [Huron] Mountains."

ashfault = asphalt

Ask the DNR = A largely Yooper program, sometimes on TV, sometimes on radio. Representatives of various DNR departments answer call-in questions from the public. They sometimes hear more speeches from callers than questions, "'cause ever' Yooper deer hunter know more den any dose punk PhDs studied cervids and whitetails dere entire lives . . . "

ass-bite = tell someone off

asschunk = adjunct

asshaul = hassle

assroots = grassroots

ass–wire = sciatic nerve

ast = asked or ask (works for either)

ATB = Above the Britch (meaning Da Big Mac, and implying da U.P.); opposite of BTB (which means Lower Michigan, and not da U.P.)

Ate 'em & Leave = Adam & Eve

audiobull = audible

audiogymnocafeterium (da audigcaf) = Multipurpose rooms available to the public in schools or government spaces.

August = Allegedly the only month that the U.P. has not gotten snow. [Author's note: I was flying one day in July, in the late 1960s, and radioed from mid–North Dakota back to our K. I. Sawyer AFB command post, south of Marquette, seeking a weather report for our scheduled landing time in a couple of hours, and heard the following: "Sir, we've got snow and blowing snow." Pregnant pause. "Say again, Control?" Pause. "Yessiree, sir, snow and blowing snow." Pause. "But she ain't sticking, sir." Be advised: You can't bring enough seasonal clothing changes for a trip to the U.P. because you never know from day to day what the weather will bring.]

B

babymama = The birth mother of a man's child, as in "Dat man so busy, 'e gotts five babymamas."

babysit = dat yella stuff in diapers

baby swamp = bog

backcountry = da woods, da boonies, da toolies, etc.

Backdoor Bettye = "Dat womyn 'roun' town, she allas ready ta come over visit."

back-lookers = rearview and sideview mirrors; also, "side-lookers"

backstraps = tastiest, most tender cut of venison

badgery = dull gray in color

bad lip = ad lib

bag = sack

Baitsbook = Facebook; "Crap in dere makes some uvda pipples really pissed, but good way keep track da pals an' chums."

Bake da lake = "Break a leg," or "Good luck"; "What ackers say each udder 'fore curtain she go oop."

bakery = Refers to all baked goods, donuts, etc. A Yooper says, "Got bakery?" and clerk answers, "Hole, or no holes?," meaning, "Donuts or something else?"

baking = begging

baku = [Finnish] Small belt or boot knife carried by Russian Finns, who in the old days were quick to use it in a fight.

Baldwin Bullshidos = A now-defunct trout-fishing gang that fished the Pere Marquette River watershed for forty marvelous years. One gang member was a Yooper from Ironwood, another, a former resident of Rudyard in Chippewa County, a third, a native Hoser-hockey player from Da Canadian Soo, and a fourth had a deep and abiding connection to people in Grand Marais in Alger County. At least three of said Bullshidos had encounters with Limpy-like persons while fishing off the grid in Da Yoop.

baldy = An antlerless female whitetail; a doe. [Author's note: There are occasionally antlered does in the deer herd . . . genetic exceptions.]

baldy Buddhastatists = "Dose guys in or'nge dresses beggin' da handouts at airports, an' handin' oot da 'oly bull."

banana beak = European starling; "Da breasts make good meat pie filler-upper."

Banana Belt = *see* "Yooper Riviera"

bandog = any vicious dog used for guard duty [Author's note: This word was in use in Shakespeare's time.]

banger = somebody with heavy fists, who likes to fight

banjolele = any small stringed instrument

banking = "Dis mean dose snowbanks in winter, how pipples piles snow 'round their houses in town an' da camps inda bush."

bar = borrow

Baragastan = what Limpy and Service call Baraga County

Baraga Yobama = Barack Obama ("If he ain't no Mooslum, he prolly Indi'n.")

bareface lie = boldface lie

Barfie doll, da = Barbie doll

barium = (pronounced "parium") Limpy tells us, "Dis what dey do wit' dead bodies."

barkin' spiders = (pronounced "parkin' spiders") Flatulence, farts, noxious gaseous hemissions (and shemissions)—issued with some élan, of course.

barley pop = (pronounced "parley bob") beer

Barry = Barry Sanders, Hall of Fame running back for the Detroit Lions. Yooper Packer fans admired him enough to grant him Yooper One-Name Fame.

barter = "How 'boot trade my crap for youse's crap?" This is the essence of underground Yooper economy, which most prizes untraceable cash (harder for IRS to keep track of).

basics = basis; "Like, what youse's basics for ta hunta deer? Da gun, da bullet, da beer, like dat."

basket buck = Think of arranging your hands so that if you move your wrists, the tips of your fingers will touch. This looks sort of like a small basket, and thus, represents a small rack of antlers on a buck.

bassoomed indecent = presumed innocent

bassooms = breasts; "Dere's two uvem on da wymyns."

bat' = bath (not required in hunting camp)

batsball = baseball

batshirt crazy = certifiably insane; "If guy t'inks bats wear shirts, he crazy!"

battle boil = fighting pitch; the fight is on; a battle royal

bayrometeer = barometer

beagle = baby eagle

beak = big

beak bucks, da = the big bucks; the bosses; big shots, head honchos

Beak Lakes = big lakes, e.g., the Great Lakes

beater = Any old vehicle; *see also* "veek." Reserved for outdoor, mostly camp use, and if run entirely on private property, it will be without state plates (*see also* "fish car").

beautyatrician = beautician

beautycussulkant = beauty consultant

beaverage = any liquid refreshment, hot, cold, with or without alcohol content

beaver-slides = skid marks in skivvies

beaves = either beavers, or beefs, depending on context

bed polka = *see* "boink"

bedsman = "Weddin' best man's job make sure bride-gloom go bed, sleep-in on hitch-up night."

beebleberry = Originally from *Little Lulu* comic strip, now used by some to refer to any berries "dat don't grow nowheres in da U.P., nor is dose ones eated onny by da birds an' da critters."

beelzeboobs = "Dose t'ings some wymyns got, might could leads youse to da Devil's Dogs."

beer = social beaverage; one of several basic Yooper food groups

beercorn = deercorn; bait

beer-faced lie = "Don't count, 'cause ev'body know dis jus' da beers talkin'."

beerocraps = bureaucrats

beer-pardon = "Give dese after da guys go hot, den cool back down."

beer-parked = not straight; crooked

beer sicken = whole chicken cooked with full beer can up its butt

beer wallah = "Dat guy gets come camp jus' 'cause allas buy, carry da beer."

beforetime = formerly; previously

beggerate = to beg

beggie = rutabaga

Belkie = Pelkie (Baraga County—oddly enough, the Finns don't pronounce Baraga "Paraga.")

betclothes = bedclothes; sheets, pillowcases, condoms, stuff like dat

betweenerity = indecisive; unable to make a decision or take direction

beyond da pail = beyond the pale; beyond the limits

Bez'mer = Bessemer, in Gogebic County; high school teams were once called the Speedboys (and nobody seems to know why!).

bezooker = [Dutch] visitor; you hear this sometimes over in the eastern U.P.

B'Hoys, Bahoys = da Irish; dose micks; da tatey-eaters

bibble = to imbibe (partake of alcoholic beverages)

Bibleback = preacher, minister

Bible barkers = extreme Christian fundamentalists

Big Girlie and/or Da Gray Lady = Lake Superior

Big Mac = Mackinac Bridge; also called Da Britch

bike = can refer to a bicycle, motorcycle (street or dirt), or an ATV/ORV

Bikings = Vikings

Bill = former Michigan governor Bill Milliken

biofuel = corn juice for cars

biparmesan = bipartisan

bipoker = bipolar; "Youse never know what card dey gone play."

birching = spanking; also a tradition (*see* "saunas")

bird-a-paradise = any exotic feathered creature; or any woman from the village of Paradise

Bird, Da = Mark "Da Bird" Fidrych, famous and eccentric Detroit Tigers pitcher who talked to baseballs and flapped around on the pitcher's mound like a wild Big Bird. Great player, dearly loved by Yoopers.

birdseye (or birdeye) maple = One of the rarest and most valuable woods in the world. Pattern is distinctive, with small eyes disrupting smooth grain lines. The cause of the patterning is not yet well understood, though there are some theories. This is hard to detect in most living maples; only when cut down does it become apparent. Such trees are immediately segregated and locked up for sale or future use. Birdseye occurs in *Acer saccharum*, and trees in the Great Lakes yield the largest number in the world. Among many other uses, birdseye and other forms of maple (burled, quilted, curly) are used to create decorative dashboards for Rolls-Royce vehicles. Something like 90 percent of the world's birdseye maple is found inside a 200-mile radius of Escanaba, mostly north of there, along the southern shore of Lake Superior.

birt' mum = birth mother; also, babymama

biscuit = hockey puck (frozen and made of vulcanized rubber) bitchreall = vitriol

blabbertising = advertising

blabble = stupid talk

blabulate = blather

black bear candy = beechnuts

Blackbilly = Black country music

blackbird storm = Very cold, unexpected storm in late spring that can bring a lot of snow. Blackbird storms kill a lot of mammals, like deer, who by late March are already overstressed by the extremes of a U.P. winter. An average winter will kill an estimated 100,000 white-tailed deer in the U.P.; a bad winter, twice that toll.

blackie = black bear (*Ursus americanus*)

blacksail = pirate, thief, ganker; also means "blackmail" to Limpy

black your face = Old trapper term, meaning to go to war against someone. Native Americans used to blacken their faces before going on raids. Hollywood turned "blackface" into Disneylike warpaint.

blag'eye piss = black-eyed peas

blagflies = Commonly called blackflies, these flying pests are actually buffalo gnats. You won't feel them bite, but the bites on some folks will quickly swell and begin to itch like the dickens. Best way to end the itch fast is to mix a little water with Adolph's Meat Tenderizer, make a little paste, and apply liberally to the itchy spot.

blag ice = Black ice; first dark, hard, smooth ice of early winter. Before subsequent temp shifts begin to cause snow to accumulate, and the winds change its character, this hard, dark ice is best for skating, as it's barren and without snow—which it won't be for most of the winter season.

blahblab = "Talkin' a lotta boring s'it."

blahblahbarians = "Jamokes speak lots words, say nuttin'."

blahblithertalk = meaningless small talk

blahbology = worthless political blabber and beliefs

blahgly = a boring, ugly day

Blambi = "Da faked robot deers da game wardens use ta snooker fools and violators."

blame blower = flame thrower

blaze = To mark a new trail, either by nicking trees, laying dead wood markers on ground, or using night-eye tacks.

bleach of contact = breach of contract; "Jus' whitewash da hull demm t'ing, yah?"

blecky = messy

blind (brush) = "Hideout on ground made outen piled-up sticks fum where youse ambush da deers."

blind (tower) = "Hideout on da stilts, she sit pret' 'igh up, ambush da deers fum high above an' way-far away."

blind (tree) = "Hideout up da tree where youse ambush da deers fum above."

blindage = piss-poor eyesight

blind shares = "Like dose time-share places."

blindsight = can't see what comes next; or hindsight

blinger = verbal "shot" at someone

blingsing = hip-hop, rap, all dat stuff

Blizzardgeddon = The worst winter storm ever in Da Yoop; "Dere's usual one storm uvda cent'ry ev'ry winner."

blogdinacious = writes down ev't'ing for da social meanies

blond drunk = blind drunk

bloobs = blueberries

blood bandits = ticks (wood ticks and deer ticks)

blood clog = blood clot

bloody = Pejorative, adjectival Yooper descriptor; da bloody truck, wife, shotgun, etc.; once a very naughty word in the English language, it's now a mild form of emphasis, roughly akin to "very," and sometimes a substitute in semi-civilized company for stronger, nastier expletives. [Author's note: A bloody useful word indeed is "bloody."]

blooey = bluebird

blow-by boat = jet ski or jet boat

blowdown = A tangle of fallen trees and brush, usually from wind, or a combination of high winds and ice.

blowfly = "Dem nasty bugs dat hatch outten dead, rottin' meat."

bluebird sky = blue, windless, sunny

blue devil sky = "Look like bluebird sky now, but trouble, she be comin' down da pike."

blue dumpies = feeling down, depressed, owly

Blue Goose = Michigan State Police cruiser; also nickname for Northwest Airlines bluegreen flu, da = Miners who escaped underground explosions back in the Keweenaw copper-mining heyday often appeared to surface with blue-green marks on their exposed skin and faces. Some caught this peculiar flu and refused to ever work underground again.

blue heat = tar melts; when you see mirages in the distance on highways and in fields

blue ice: The sapphire-ish ice chunks found in the roots of shaded cedar roots in swamps, sometimes extending into June and July. Think glacier-colored ice, "wit' all da air squeezened oot." This term, ironically, also applies to human waste that freezes when ejected from aircraft at high altitudes. I know . . . TMI.

bluejay sky = windy, blustery gray, angry

blue lagoony = blue loogey; "Dis what youse spit when drink too much."

blunt dog = a very dull fellow

BMBB! = Bring Me Bloody Beer!

boar's nest = an untidy, filthy, unkempt camp, or house

boat anger = Boat anchor; anything highly impractical and bound to fail; for example, electric vehicles. "No place in Yoop ta plug in da demm t'ings. Where dey gone go? Dey'll all end up as da boat angers."

boatuvus, da = the both of us

BOB (Blaze Orange Brigade) = annual invasion of downstate and out-of-state hunters

bodderhood = botherhood (meaning, brotherhood)

bog orange = potato

Bohunk = any foreigner, though this term initially meant immigrants from central Europe

Bohunkian = any foreign language

boink = coitus; intercourse

boinkouvelard = Lovers Lane

boinkubine = concubine

Bojo = Good morning or good day (*Bonjour, en français*); this shortened slang version is now a traditional Ojibwa (Anishinaabe) greeting.

Bolarus = Polaris, the North Star. [Author's note: Polaris is always situated between the outer lip of the Big Dipper and the Chair of Cassiopeia, which until the 1930s astronomers called Cassiopeia's Chair, and since have been calling it Cassiopeia the Queen, but in USAF Undergraduate Navigator Training (UNT) at Mather AFB in Sacramento, California, in 1965–1966, the Air Force apparently never got the memo. It was referred to there (for reasons unknown, or, to be fair, unrecalled by me) as the Chair of Cassiopeia, and I still call it that. Some lessons forged early, last long. Also, "Dat Bolarus is company makin' da snowmobiles an' da ATV side-by-each youse an' youse's girl took outen ta da toolies for da boinkin'."]

boldiful = bold, audacious

bolters = runners, escapees, cowards, absconders

bombing barn = outhouse

bonebox = mouth

bonehanded = barehanded

Bonniejo = Limpy's friendly greeting, a peculiar form of *Bonjour*

boobler = bubbler; public water fountain

Boobopolis = any hick town

booger sprouts = nose hairs

book-eater = scholar

book of Jesuscyst = book of Genesis

boomerang = booming, going well; "Dat bar up dere in Rock, she goin' boomerang, eh."

Booners = Animals—which possess certain qualities—taken by hunters that are then officially "scored" by qualified persons. The Boone and Crockett Club is an American nonprofit organization that advocates fair chase hunting in support of habitat conservation. The specimens that meet the organization's requirements qualify for Boone and Crockett world ratings and rankings. Various outdoor and hunting shows will pay Booner owners to bring their prizes to shows for display, and to share the story of how they bagged it.

boonies, da = As in "da boondocks" or "da toolies"; "somewheres way oot dere in da deep woods."

Booze-over-Bible = more bars and taverns than churches in the U.P.

borrow-me = loan to me; or "Can I use that . . . ?"

bosh = rubbish, nonsense, offal

bosky = wooded

bough bed = Mainly used by loggers, but a technique used in some hunting camps, too. Make bed frame of eight-inch logs. Then cut twigs that are ten to twelve inches long and stand them on end, densely packed, with a slight lean to the head of the bed. Continue stacking the smaller pieces, working down toward the foot of the bed. When finished, unroll the bedroll from the foot upward, toward the head of the bed. A lot of work, but worth the effort. Such beds are durable and have considerable spring to them.

bountree = bounty; "Cash da State usta pay for killin' pesky t'ings."

bourbon = burden

bowler-yard = boulevard

boxcow = store-boughten beef

Bozart = musician, artist; a form of the French term *beaux-arts*

bracken = ferns

brain-bomb = syphilis

brain bucket = helmet, or just a hat

brainclouds = rain clouds; confused, unsure

braincured = softheaded; not too swift a thinker

brainfarse = brain fart; any memory lapse, failure to recall something

brain of salt = grain of salt

brain rocket = any psychedelic or other drug that ignites/affects the central nervous system

brainsqueezeler = mind-bender; something difficult to think through

brandy = human liquid fuel for long rides on snowmobiles, four-wheelers, etc.; or for any other outdoor activity

brangle = to squabble noisily

brassy ass = haughty, stuck-up, egotistical

breedbate = troublemaker, instigator

brekkie = breakfast

britch = bridge

Britch, Da = The Bridge

brizzle = to scorch or singe

broke parts = people with disabilities

brookie = (*Salvinus fontanalis*) Slang for brook trout, which is actually a char, not a trout. Also called in various parts of North America a squaretail, speckled trout (specs), brook charr, and mud trout. Great eating! If you are of the Yooper School of Catch and Release, into grease, try this: a pinch of brown sugar before you pan-fry 'em.

brottel = brothel; Limpy confuses it for bushel, as in "Dat jamoke hide 'is light under the brottel."

brown sugar = sugar sand (soft, bad for da fish cars); "An' sugar, she ain't so good for da ticker, neither-either."

browse = nosh, food; "Any grub animal munch on, like tatey chips an' pretzels for humans."

browse line = The line about eight to ten feet in the air on cedar trees that marks the highest point the animal can stretch up their necks and on their hind legs nibble cedar tips in winter. [Author's note: These lines are very visible to passing motorists and their passengers.]

brushhog (or bushhog) = Implement used to clear heavy under-growth in trail construction or clearing spaces around buildings, or along the edges of fields, or food plots.

brush wolf = (*Canis latrans*) coyote. The term is specific to the *very* large Yooper coyotes which tend to grow quite a bit larger than coyotes BTB. As a general rule, zoologists tell us mammals increase in size in more northern habitats. There also may have been some cross-breeding with wolves by Yooper coyotes. The coyote is closely related to, but smaller than, eastern gray and red wolves.

BTB = Below the Bridge (meaning the Mackinac Bridge that connects the U.P. with Lower Michigan)

bub = Bulb and/or breast; also a sort of sarcastic greeting (e.g., "Hey dere, Bub"). Or, as Limpy starts to complain to some cop about some ticket he's about to be given, the cop holds up his hands and says, "Tell it to da jutch, Bub." (Thanks to Miss Anna Torsky for this quip, shared with me over the family breakfast when she was ten-ish.)

buck = male white-tailed deer or male snowshoe hare

Buck Bay = nickname for Dollar Bay, Houghton County

Buck Nystrom = There are lots of bucks in Da Yoop—restaurants, stores, etc.—but only one "Buck." The late Buck Nystrom was a longtime football player, coach, and local businessman in Marquette. Fished in the same ratty hippers most of his adult life. Never met a stranger, even in da woods. Great guy, missed by many.

bucketball = basketball

buck fever = "Dis da temporary case da shaky-jake nerves make da hunter ta miss badly even on da layup shots." The disorder can be applied to virtually any situation requiring self-control and steady nerve. The term is loosely equivalent to "operator failure."

buck-fisted = left-handed

Buck Law = This law, instituted in the early twentieth century, required hunters to shoot male deer with visible horns before female deer. Many hunters mistakenly think it had something to do with genetics, when in fact it was put in place because so many hunters were shooting each other, non-hunting civilians, and animals other than white-tailed deer. When old-timers talk about what great hunters they were, this is pure bull. The safety stats from the early twentieth century reveal they were unbelievably incompetent, compared to later in the century, or even now.

buckskins = Hides turned into clothes, favored by trappers in the olden days, and hippies in the more recent past. Naturally light color can be darkened by smoking the hide over an open fire.

buckstore = "Onny place can get da buck—oot dere inna woods where da deers live."

buckular dystrophy = A social disorder that affects mostly males, who want to kill and talk about nothing but bucks with trophy-size antlers. Perhaps an odd form of OCD.

bug juice = insect repellent; *see* "DEEP (DEET)"

bugle = mating call of a bull elk in fall rutting season

bullet-proof snow = "Snow wit' da hard crust."

bullface lie = baldface lie

bull moose or paddlehead = male moose

bumblejumble = a messy problem or situation

bum riding = *see* "hooking"

buncha = a whole lot

bunglebee = bumblebee; "Youse seen dose t'ings fly? Don't know where dey go next, eh."

bun mouse = Someone with a sweet tooth, especially for cinnamon rolls and certain Finnish pastries.

bunnyhugger = Pejorative term for people who seem to give more priority to nonhumans than to humans; over-the-top animal worshippers.

burning daylight = Wasting time; oddly, this term seems to first appear not in the U.P. but in two of William Shakespeare's plays, *Romeo and Juliet* and *The Merry Wives of Windsor*.

bush, da real = "Da jungle over dere to Halfrica."

bush bunnies = Attractive women (usually nubile and young) who grow up in da bush and sometimes show up at local taverns, which then creates . . . situations.

bushcuts = short haircuts; e.g., brushcut, flattop, whitewaller

bush pop = Mix a little vinegar and a spoon of sugar in a glass of water. Before drinking, mix in a quarter teaspoon of baking soda.

bushvets = War veterans who move to the backwoods after they return. Usually these folks are extreme loners, but sometimes they "gather" in "villages"—small clusters of huts or cabins with folks who've had similar experiences and reactions to them. Many suffer from severe post-traumatic stress disorder (PTSD).

bushwah = bullshit

bushway = (pronounced "Booshway") Trapper term, from the French *bourgeois*. Referred to company men responsible for indentured trappers who were forced by their circumstances to work for fur company monopolies. In a general sense, the word means the man in charge.

bushwhack = to go off-piste, or off-trail; to go where other humans don't often go; also, to ambush someone

butcherbird = (*Lanius borealis*) Also called loggerheads or northern shrikes, these small birds impale their prey—often while still alive—on spikes, thorns, or barbed wire, and leave them there for days, or weeks. They attack humans with their beaks and are relentless and aggressive. [Author's note: I think this would be a great name for pro, college, or high school sports teams.]

but-firsts = "Youse go do dis one t'ing, and t'ink but first, den go do dat t'ing, which remind you do nudder t'ing, and by den youse forgetted what dat first t'ing was, and she don't never get done."

butt-logic = "When talk an' t'ink come fum way sout' da brain."

button buck = young male whitetail with antlers barely showing

buttriloquist = "Pipples talk outen dere asses."

buttsgill = buzz kill

butt-shave = close call; near miss

bydagrades a Gott = by the grace of God

bymotor compression = bipolar depression; "Youse know, when da wymyns kisses youse all over an' dis feel so good, seems like youse's teet's'll blow up!"

C

cackle or cluck or clucker or sicken = chicken

cackleberry salad = egg salad

cackle breath or sicken breath = chicken broth

cacks or cackleberries = eggs

cadaverlac = hearse

caffeetes = "Dose jamokes like da fancy muds an' joes."

caffeinds or caffreakoids = coffee addicts

cag = gag

cagmag = really bad food

cakey = soft, meek, mild-mannered

Callun Pyle Chen'ral, dat = the late General Colin Powell, former
secretary of state

calvary = cavalry (a lot of Americans make this swap)

Camelaro = Chevy Camaro

camelflesh or cameraflage = camouflage

Camp = That place in the woods or outside town where Yoopers go
to wreckreate; called cottages and/or vacation homes downstate. If
everyone is there for deer hunting, the camp becomes Deer Camp;
if for fishing, Fish Camp; if for bird hunting, Bird Camp. If for
drinking and carousing, "Camp" suffices.

camp-deer = Years ago, Michigan deer camps were legally entitled
to shoot a "community" deer whose meat would feed all the
mouths in camp, which was often for the full two weeks of the
November firearms deer season. This allowance was later dis-
continued by regulation, but has at least once in recent memory
been reenacted. Hunters need to read their deer hunting regs to
know if it's on or off in any given year. The reg is still in effect
in some other states. Half a decade ago, many deer camps were
filled with generations of relatives, with the old ones arriving
first before the season to scout, set up old surplus military tents,
cut firewood, and take care of other chores to prepare for the
younger generations to subsequently arrive to spend time hunting in the family group.

campfire culture = Campfires and woodstove fires are regular features
of Yooper life, which makes it useful to have some familiarity
with some of the terms. These will get you started, but it's not an
exhaustive list. There are separate entries for these terms later in
this collection, but I wanted to help you sort them out relatively
in one place, so: *halko* = [Finnish] a log, three-feet-plus long (one

meterish); *klapi* = [Finnish] firewood piece smaller than a *halko*; *pilke* = [Finnish] firewood piece smaller than a *klapi* (the order then, from largest to smallest, is *halko, klapi, pilke*); *ronga* = [Finnish] huge chunk of wood; *runko* = [Finnish] tree trunk. It is likely that the term *ronga* was derived somehow from *runko*. When one pronounces *ronga*, one has to drop the voice, roll the "r" harshly, and say, "T'row for da fire to me dat RRROWNGGA!"

Canadian crapkicker or Alberta clipper = Limpy prefers the first term.

canklesore = canker sore

cannibal = Term for individuals hailing from particularly remote and lawless areas. Cannibals are said to eat their young, meaning to lack all normal feelings and emotions. Never a compliment.

Canucks (or Hosers or Funnel Heads or Puck-Eaters) = Anyone hailing from Canada.

cape = The hide covering the head, neck, and fore-shoulders of a game animal, usually a large mammal, often removed for trophy mounts, or for other decorative use.

car house = garage (pronounced "grudge" or "grutch")

car muffs = tarps

Carphard = Carhartt line of work clothes

carpoo' = carpool

Carp River Codge = Carp River College, local slang for Marquette Prison

carpuncle-neutered = carbon-neutral

carputer = the computer in your car or truck

cashbox = home bank; "Why I given moneys ta some jamokes in da banks?"

Cash Laundry = Michigan Lottery

cashnoseeum or cashego'way = casino

cash-wall, da = ATM

castratenauts = celibates

CAT = Popular name for methcathinone, a form of methamphetamine (speed) that's very addictive and dangerous. Parke-Davis had the patents for this in 1957, and included a "recipe" in the literature in 1954. Some U of M students discovered this and cooked up a batch, sharing it with pals, and the whole thing took off from there, starting in the U.P. but spreading. Dis called Da Yoop's own designer drug. It is a chemical cousin of both methamphetamine and the Somali khat plant. CAT is relatively easy to make from readily available ingredients that range from paint thinner to lye. And it's cheap to cook. It is powerful, intensely habit-forming, and can often lead to paranoia, extreme weight loss, bloody noses, and loss of sleep. "Very nasty s'it," according to Limpy. The bulk of users used to be in Michigan, Indiana, and Wisconsin, although not so much anymore. The drug has made scattered appearances in Washington State, Colorado, Montana, Idaho, and Virginia. In nearly every case, the people involved seemed to have had some sort of connection to Michigan's Upper Peninsula.

catamount = mountain lion or cougar

catch-and-release = The practice of releasing rather than killing fish, pioneered in amateur and pro bass fishing circles many years ago, and subsequently adopted for other species, such as trout.

catch-and-release . . . into grease = Yooper iteration of catch-and-release; "It's all about da food, stoopid!"

catchitallpot = crock pot

catchpoll = dogcatchers; animal control pipples

Catchus Clay = Cassius Clay, da best scrapper *ever*

Catlick = Roman Catholic; "Dey're all over Da Yoop, eh?"

catspaw = dupe

caviar fish = sturgeon

cawcawpony = cacophony; "Noise fum buncha dem crows!"

Cedar Savage or Ridgerunner or Wood Tick = All terms for those Yoopers who prefer to live remotely, as in off the grid (in Limpy's pronunciation: "offendagrit").

cedar swamp = A special habitat that teems with life, and in winter serves as thermal cover for white-tailed deer. Expect to find a mix of tamarack (larch), black spruce, northern white cedar, or white pine, balsam fir, eastern hemlock, and a few hardwoods, such as black ash. Michigan has by some estimates four million acres of cedar swamps, and if you've ever been lost or turned around in one on a cloudy day or in a good snow, it seems like the state is *all* cedar swamps. Typically, there is an overgrown, interlaced canopy above and nasty, exposed roots on the ground. Provides great thermal cover for deer in our severe northern winters. Being unknown ground (*Terra incognita*), one who gets lost in such places has had a bout of Temporary Undisorientation. [Author's note: I *love* cedar swamps.]

Cee-Ess-Ess (CSS) = Can't See Shit; *see* "whiteout"

cellar savers or basement savers = Volunteer fire departments; volunteer firefighters in Da Yoop are greatly admired for their courage, if not for their uniform fire-extinguishing skills. Volunteer groups here generally don't have the amount or frequency of technical training typical of volunteer fire units in, e.g., Upstate New York.

cellphony = smartphone addict

cement highway = any hard-surfaced road

cementia = dementia

cents of hummers = sense of humor

C'est vrai = [French] (pronounced *Say vray*) It's true.

chaffer = to bargain or dicker

chain saw = a tool in every Yooper's truck and camp

chalk = American woodcock feces; *see* "timberdoodle"

chalkwall = blackboard

champaign = flat country

change-quick youse's oil = vomit/puke

Channing = A town in north Dickinson County, near where wolves were last seen in the 1960s, and subsequently rediscovered by DNR wildlife biologist (and former conservation officer) Jim Hammill to be repopulating the area, circa 1989. Despite stubborn poaching and some indiscriminate killing, the population has been steadily increasing ever since then.

Chassells = Yum-yum, eat 'em up! Domestic variety of wonderfully sweet strawberries grown in Houghton County. Get 'em in June. [Author's note: Chassell is a town in Houghton County, eight to ten miles south of the city of Houghton.]

cheapsteak = cheapskate

cheapytinky = anything manufactured by cheap labor outside the United States

checkheimers = A unique, but not unknown, brain malfunction; "Forget ta write down da checks youse wrote in town."

checkturds or chenkers = checkers

cheesehead or cheesie = Wisconsin native or resident

cheeseskinner = cheapskate

Cheesus = Jesus

cheetodust = something worthless; Fool's Gold

chenitalsmen = gentlemen

chentile = gentle

Cherman brown trout = (*Salmo trutta*) These transplanted fish were widely known as German brown trout in the United States until World Wars I and II. Then, because of PC in the air, not so much. Now they're more commonly known as just brown trout.

chermancide = germicide; "Mightaoughtamebbeshouldacoulda used some'a cherms [germs], microbes, viruses, all dat stuff can't see, in da big war, on dose demm Chermans."

chess-waders = chest waders

chest = chess; "Dat demm 'ard game; radder play da checkturds, red-blacks, wah!"

chickchack = chitchat

Chiclet mechanic = dentist

Chiclets = teeth

chillery = hidey-hole, hideout; "Da place where youse can go till da heat, she go down."

chillmidity = humidity, cool air, dampness

chinchers = bedbugs

Chinese rack = Any large set of deer antlers with an extensive number of points. Also may refer to any asymmetrical or nontypical set of antlers.

chin holes or chin dents = dimples

Chinky chenkers = Chinese checkers

Chinook = (*Oncorhynchus tshawytscha*) king salmon; or a warm spring wind

chip of fools = ship of fools

Chippewa, Chippeway = Ojibwa Indians, who call themselves Anishinaabe. The Ojibwa, the Ottawa (Odawa), and the Potawatomi tribes are all members of the Council of Three Fires. In parts of Canada the Cree are also related to the Ojibwa. [Author's note: The word *Chippewa* has an interesting history. The first Europeans encountered the Anishinaabe (pronounced something like *Nish-NAH-beh*, which is what they call themselves, and means The People). The French seemed to shorten this to Nishnawbe, and the English ear heard Chippeway, or Otchipwe, which eventually became Ojibwe, which morphed over time in English into Ojibwa. In Indian histories, we find that almost all tribes refer in their own language to themselves as The People, or the Human Beings, and people not of the tribe as Other, or worse . . . But for most other tribes not considered our bosom buds, we refer to them with terms such as Snakes or something considered less than human.] *See also* "Council of Three Fires."

chirrupies = bats

chit or s'it = shit

chitteries, da = There's no known word for this phenomenon, which sometimes hits some dogs when they happen upon certain scents. The dog immediately freezes up, focuses on the smell, and begins to drool, shake, and blink wildly. Vets don't have a name for it, but it's real, and, oddly enough, it hits Limpy too for reasons unknown—perhaps excitement over danger or prospects of something good. Who knows?

chixchax = womyntalk; chitchat

chocobobo = Nightcap comprised of hot dark chocolate with a sploomph of bourbon (bobo). [Author's note: Quaffed this beauty in mid-Menominee County, but it seems likely to be an imported delicacy.]

choke = joke

chokecherries = Wild cherries growing on small to large trees; the fruit is a favored food of wildlife, especially birds and black bears. Whitetails browse on the leaves in late autumn.

chompsticks = chopsticks

chook, chuke, toque = All of these terms refer to a woolen (sock) hat favored by many Yoopers, males and females, year-round, and oddly enough, a lot of rappers, as well.

choppers = These winter mittens / snowmobile gauntlets tend to have extended length; they were wool- or fur-lined in da olden days, and are now warmed by more modern insulating materials.

"chort roll inna long crass" = quickie outdoor boink

chrome = A term for silvery steelhead, freshly up the river from a larger water body.

chuck-knuck = Someone odious, a schemer; a fool's blend of chuck-lehead and knucklehead.

chum = buddy, pal, friend

churchlite = "When pipples go church onny when feels like it—not every week."

ciddyit, shiddyit, siddit, siddyot, chittyot = Anyone from any city, anywhere. [Author's note: No standards in this for, or definition of, "city" are provided by Yoopers, but my guess is that anything larger than Marquette or Escanaba would probably qualify.]

ciddyit work duds = "Suit, tie, dresses, all dat silly s'it."

circusized = circumsized

clabber = mud and muck

clapped-out = tricked-out, fancy

clapper-whacker = door-knocker

clapstander = standing ovation

Clareavoydance = "Youse don't never want dance wit' dat Clare womyn. She a bloodsucker an' a real pip."

claws = fingernails

cleancut = clearcut, heavily logged forest area; may also refer to a shave

cleanup crews = looters

clear and peasant dagger = clear and present danger

cliffy = cliff swallow

clinchpoop = a jerk

clip = magazine for a firearm

clodic = clumsy, awkward

close-lookers = eyeglasses; magnifying glass

clucks, cluckers = chickens

coagalator = calculator; also cackalator

coasters = Brook trout that live in the Great Lakes and spawn in rivers; they grow much larger than brookies that spend their lives in rivers and creeks. They were once quite plentiful in the Great Lakes, but not so much anymore.

Coastie = current or former member of the US Coast Guard

cockabulldog = head honcho, bossman, guy in charge

codge = college

coffinbait = the terminally ill

coinkydoinks = coincidence

coitus downdaroadus = to elope

coldening = The weather is getting cold.

cold flush = gold rush

collywobbles, or da fast-moving poop = diarrhea (industrial-strength)

come-along = tow straps; standard truck gear up here (along with jumper cables)

come-behind, da = trailer

comefar = a foreigner, immigrant, or stranger from afar

come-hit-on-me-look = come-hither look

community chest, da = "Dat would be Louise over to da Dew Duck Inn."

complexicate = complicate

condamn = condemn

conflaggerate = conflagrate

confooled = confused

Confusion = Confucius; "Youse know, dat Shina guy say all dose stoopid t'ings like da wymyns dat fly downside up, dey gone crack up? Dat guy."

congenitals = credentials

conkers = "When youse come in dead tired, flop down da chair, go quick-fast sleep, youse gone conkers."

conkflaggerate = To use a flagpole (with or without) a flag as weapon in a barroom brawl, or public disturbance. [Author's note: Like those jamokes at the Capitol on January 6, 2021.]

conkonnanut = coconut

conscript = concept

conservation officer = A modern title for Michigan's game wardens, although unlike some of their historical predecessors, modern COs are fully empowered peace officers with the same powers as the State Police, and often federally deputized as well. Older Yoopers, especially old-time violators, often still call COs da game wardens.

consternative = conservative

cooked bread = toast

cooked water = boiled water

cook iron = griddle

Copper Country, Da = Term for the area with copper-bearing ore, which stretches roughly northeast from just west of Ontonagon around White Pine, all the way north and east up to Copper Harbor, at the tip of the Keweenaw Peninsula. Long ago, Indians mined copper on Isle Royale as well, which is just off the tip of Da *KEY-vin-aw* (the way it's pronounced by lifelong locals).

Copper Country Shuffle = Slipping and sliding on the ice; term can be used for the typical motion and unbalanced awkwardness of winter outdoor walking anywhere in Da Yoop.

corks = caulked (steel-spiked) boots

corner office = coroner's office

corn on da cop = corn on the cob

costard = old-timer's term for apple

cottontail deer = What some downstater or out-of-stater greenhorn once called white-tailed deer. Limpy is *still* bemoaning this example of nature ignorance.

Coughis or Covis, da = COVID-19

Council of Three Fires = Confederation of Michigan's three main Indian tribes: Chippewa (Ojibwa), Ottawa (Odawa), and Potawatomi. All speak Algonquin languages, which are very closely related.

coundinky = county

cousin = cozen; to trick, scam, mislead

Cousington = Baragastanian slang for Covington (Baraga County)

Cousin Jack or Jenny = Male or female hailing from Cornwall in England.

Cowablonda! = Exclamation over seeing an attractive blond.

Cowgarry = Calgary; "Cowgarry, up dere Alberta Canuckland, but not dat village sout'a L'Anse."

c'owlse = Derogatory term used to chide ciddyits: "When dey t'ink dey hearin' da owlse at night, it just some stinky old cow."

cow s'it = cow shit, cow pie, cow flop

Coxey's Army = In the old days, when red plaid was *de rigueur* for hunters. This term referred to the red-clad deer-hunting army that invaded the Yoop every November, either driving in from Wisconsin, or taking the car ferry north from Mackinaw City to Iggy [St. Ignace], with waiting hunters sometimes backed up twenty to thirty miles (sometimes as far south as Indian River) while waiting for a place on one of the boats.

coyote snack = any and all kittycats

crabdacious = capacious

crackdarocks = explosives; explains Limpy, "Da Tannerite, she give a bigger kick den most crackdarocks."

crackerjack = nifty

cradio = da car radio

cranes = crayons

crap = crab; "Last night we went ooten to da gasino for da crap dinners."

crapapples = crabapples

crapes = grapes

crapids = rapids

crapital = Capital or capitol; Limpy uses the word for either and both.

crapovino = cheap wine (think Two-Buck Chuck and the like)

craptacious = not so good, shitty; also means capacious, as in a whole lot of something

crawl-and-creep = recon; to physically check out a place

creased peg = greased pig

creepatures = creatures

creeper or crawler gear = the lowest gear range in 4WD

creepin' whiteout = "Kind sneaks up on youse before youse know it."

creepy-jeepies = heebie-jeebies

crematoaste = creosote

crew = "Gang a chuck-knucks violates togedder." Can be a formal or informal, spur-of-the-moment assemblage.

cribbage = The national card game of Yooper hunting camps, eh; *see also* "takin' wood."

crick = creek

crick-mud = "Smear youse's face wit' dis gunk as sunblock or as prepellent."

crimeogenticks = cryogenics

crimpy = trapper term for a very, very cold day

Cripes! = Polite Yooper euphemism for "Christ!"; also how some Yoopers pronounce "gripes."

cripple = a wounded bird

cripple ball = crystal ball

Criteshake = for Christ's sake

critter = any living creature other than *Homo sapiens*

crittergrub = suet (pronounced *suit*) "Dis da stuff for feeds da birdies, da squrls, an' sometimes dose pesky bears, too."

cronk = fixed, set, predetermined

croodle = stick together; safety in numbers; herd mentality

crooked = deformed

crop spray or crop dusting = "To fartate whilst youse're walkin 'roun' town or inside da camp."

crotch rocket = low-slung motorcycle

crotchsniffers = wrestlers

crow hair = means, fake, scam, b.s.; "Dere ain't no such t'ing."

crunchtime = When the temp is near 0 degrees Fahrenheit, the snow gets loud underfoot.

crustine = dog-skinned (thick-skinned)

cuck = to defecate

Cuckoo Clux Clan = KKK; "Buncha jamokes run 'roun' in dere mum's sheets. In oldy days dese fools usta meet, burn crosses on Keyvinaw Bay, at site now is da State Park."

cudighi = (pronounced *COO-dih-ghee*) Homemade Yooper spicy Italian sausage usually in patty style, most often found in western Yoop; many different recipes and/or formulae.

cultelet = little cult; "Dey all da same, yah? Whackerjobs."

curly wolf = Trapper term for a man who can talk the talk *and* walk the walk. The real deal.

curvyful = buttocks; da curvy parts

cute lil clippies = cuticle clippers

cymballisdation = civilization

D

da = the

Da Beak Lake = Refers to the "Big Lake," meaning any of the Great Lakes touching the U.P.; which one depends on where you are in the U.P. (Lakes Superior, Michigan, and Huron all touch the U.P.).

Da Bird = Mark Fidyrich; tall, curly-headed Detroit Tigers pitcher, who used to stand on the mound, talk to the ball during games, and flap around like Big Bird. He was greatly beloved by Yoopers for his enthusiasm, candor, and eccentricities, not to mention his ability to throw blazing fastballs and wicked curves.

Da Britch = Mackinac Bridge, connecting Michigan's Lower Peninsula with its Upper Peninsula

Da Bush = boondocks, deep woods, wilderness

Da Captain = This title shall forever be the property of former Red Wing great Steve Yzerman.

Da Club = Urine Mound Club (Huron Mountain Club); very exclusive, 100-plus years old, with its own security force; located north of Big Bay in northernmost Marquette County.

Da Codge = The college; refers to any university, four-year college, or two-year community college that is closest—and most familiar—to a particular area.

Da Devil's Dogs = the Devil's doors

Da Dog = Yellow Dog River, north of Marquette, up toward Big Bay; great trout fishery.

Da Dog House = Greyhound bus station

Da *Fitzgerald* = The SS *Edmund Fitzgerald* was a Great Lakes freighter that sank in Lake Superior, north of Whitefish Point, during a storm on November 10, 1975, losing her entire crew of twenty-nine men. When launched on June 7, 1958, she was the largest ship on the Great Lakes, and she remains the largest to have sunk there. She was found in deep water on November 14, 1975, by a US Navy aircraft detecting magnetic anomalies, and discovered afterward to be in two large chunks. Gordon Lightfoot wrote a hit song about the wreck, which you will hear *incessantly* in various parts of the Yoop.

Da Gipper = George Gipp, the All-American football player for Notre Dame, native of Laurium, Michigan, in the Keweenaw, side by next with Red Jacket (now called Calumet). Famous movie: Ronnie Reagan played Da Gipper.

Da Island = The Island. For most folks in Michigan, this means Mackinac Island in the Straits of Mackinac. But depending on where you live in the Yoop, it can mean Drummond Island, located at the easternmost tip of the Yoop across from Detour, or it may be Grand Island in the bay off Munising in Alger County. Or it could be Isle Royale off the tip of the Keweenaw Peninsula (closer to Canada than to us).

Da Luge = "Some kinda sled race at da 'lympics"; or, "A deluge/shitload a somepin'."

Da Mitt = The approximate shape of Lower Michigan (not to be confused with Senator Mitt Romney, R-UT). Contrary to the wild speculations of some conspiracy theorists, the honorable senator, although born here when his dad was governor, was not named for this geographic feature of the Winter Wonderland.

Da Pack = The Green Bay Packers, the Yoop's most popular pro football team, though da Bears (Shitcongo), da Vikes (Minnie Soda), and even da sad-sack Lions (Destroyt) have some fans up here. Green Bay is the smallest city in the country to support a National Football League franchise, and even the gnarliest of Wood Ticks find their way to a TV to watch weekly games.

Da Porkies = "Mountains" in the Porcupine Wilderness State Park Area in the far western U.P.

Da Soo = Sault Ste. Marie (Chippewa County). When you refer to the Soo, you need to distinguish between Da Soo, which is on the south Michigan side of the St. Mary's River, and Soo, Canada, which is on the north side of the river in Ontario. [Author's note: This Soo thing can drive newcomers wacky. *Sault* is pronounced "Soo," so if you teach yourself to just say Soo, you'll do fine. *Sault* is *not* pronounced like some off-balance version of "salt."]

Da Soo Locks = The St. Mary's River locks are in Sault Ste. Marie (Da Soo). These water elevators help raise or lower shipping up to or down from Lake Superior to the lower Great Lakes. Ships come from all the Great Lakes, turning up the St. Mary's River at Detour and continuing north to the locks. [Author's note: Lake Superior is higher in elevation than all the other Great Lakes, ergo, its name in French—*Superieur*—which doesn't mean "better," only higher, or above. Though in most Yooper minds, it's not just better, but the best, eh.]

Da Yoop = The Homeland. [Author's note: In my experience, "Da Yoop" is a relatively "recent" term for the Upper Peninsula. It did not exist when I graduated from Rudyard High School (Chippewa County) in 1961. Nor did I hear it while assigned as a navigator to the USAF's 46th Air Refueling Squadron at K. I. Sawyer AFB, 1966–1970.]

Da Yoopers = The most famous, creative, and versatile Upper Peninsula musical group; youse can buy dere mukesick discs all over Da Yoop, an' BTB too.

Da Yooper Snow-Shuffle = How one walks (flat-footed) on slippery, snowy, icy areas wherever Yoopers live; they have a local name for it, e.g., Da Rudyard shuffle, da Faithhorn shuffle, etc.

damagement = damage management

Damn Near Russian = A not-so-complimentary (but clever) term for the DNR (Michigan's Department of Natural Resources). The term is used venomously by some Michigan citizens, especially in the Yoop, where game wardens historically have been seen as something between a semi-friendly foe and an out-and-out enemy.

dan, den = than and then

dance hall = place where grouses or timberdoodles do dere matin' dances

darker den inside da cow = very dark; equivalent of Oh-dark thirty

dark house = kind of tent set up on ice to spear da fishies in winter

dartbait = cork board

dat = that

daughter-law = daughter-in-law; same for son-law (son-in-law), etc.

dawgle = dawdle

dayclean = dawn

daynight = twilight; either end of the day

dead roadkill = Example of the Yooper tendency toward word re-
dundancy (*see* "roadkill").

deadrock = tombstone

deadswords = obituary

dead tire = dead tired

deadtrees = any newspaper or magazine

deasil = follow the sun east to west

deathscrecence = remains; "da stinka deat'"

decoration = declaration

Decoration of Independents = Declaration of Independence

decushions of glandular = delusions of grandeur

dee-bag = douche bag

DEEP = DEET. "Dat prepellent youse sprays or rubs on youse's skin
fore go oot, so she kills da skeets an' udder stuff." Also called bug
juice an' bug dope. Some concoctions contain DEET, and others
claim only "natural substances" (which largely be mostly placebo-
genic in mechanism of action, and effectiveness). [Author's note:
My doctor once told me: "With all the spreadable diseases now
being carried by insects in the U.P., you are *far* safer bathing daily
in DEET than risking the diseases borne by the bites."]

deep-six = shit-can, discard, get rid of

deer candy = hostas

deer drive = Usually for later in the season; some hunters abandon
individual blinds and flush the deer toward other stationary hunters
waiting to intercept. Very similar to the traditional Indian hunting
method for deer.

deerfly = bitey, annoying, pesky little yellowish devils

deer pellets = Whitetail excrement; much discussed and debated sign of deer diet, movement, and predictions for season ahead.

deer rifle = The classic was the lever-action, Model 94 Winchester .30-30. For years, the typical Michigan deer rifle in the U.P. featured a short barrel, which was far easier to maneuver in the heavy cover of cedar swamps, and along river bottomlands.

deer run = A trail with regular deer traffic wearing a visible path through and across varied terrain (various fields, woods, cedar swamps, river bottomlands, etc.).

dem = them

demm = damn

Democraps / Democramps = Democrats

demozzley = furry, bushy

devict = evict; cast someone out

dewdropper = A person who works or plays all night, then sleeps all day. This term is not a compliment, albeit dipped in a little tad bit of green-eyed envy for such a lifestyle.

dickscussion = discussion

dickstating = dictating

diddlehunting = "Go bar hunt for da hookups."

digatalkative = detective; also dickatective; "Most time da dicks is real good talkers, listen real good. Dey all diggers, dese, eh."

digger = To take a spill or untimely fall, usually caused by black ice, too much alcohol, or a combination of the two.

diggins = trapper term for the home shack or cabin

dink = anything disappointingly small

dinkdater = dictator

Dintdey? = Didn't they?

Dinty? = Didn't he?

dipping = Using long-handled net, trash can, or any other receptacle to dip smelt when they are in spawning runs up freezing cold creeks in the spring.

Dirtroit = Detroit; many Michiganders, especially those living in other parts of the state, far from the city, pronounce it DEE-troit. These folks also call it Detwat and Destroyt.

dirtstar = anus

dis = this

disfortunate = unfortunate

disguisers = undercover, plainclothes cops

dishonorary discharge = Limpy's term for dishonorable discharge. He also sometimes refers to this as an undesirable decharge.

diskmexic = dyslexic

disordid = old and nasty

disorientainted = disoriented

dispromote = to be passed over for a promotion at work, or to be demoted

distird da piece = "Dis what happen youse come ooten to da camper too early."

disuninformed = Probably means uninformed, but the meaning and usage seem to vary.

disunremember = Huh?

dis year's SOTC = the annual Storm of the Century, or epoch

divoricate = take exception to

DNA = "Dat stuff aboot tight jeans or somepin'."

DNR = The Michigan Department of Natural Resources, once called the Conservation Department. To most civilians, conservation officers (law enforcement division) *are* the DNR, and little distinction is made between DNR functions. A lot of Yoopers complain about all things with state (and/or federal) control, and often say DNR means "Damn Near Russian," which is only partially a joke.

do = Have, take, want; as in "What youse drinkin'?" Answer: "I'd do a Diet Pepsi." Sometimes this response is combined with "could," as in "I could do a Pick Axe Blonde [a brand of ale]."

do a Jimmy / do a Hoffa = disappear without a trace

dobber or daubber = bobber [Author's note: This may have something to with floats, as in the gas tanks of a motor vehicle, but the etymology of this is vague.]

dodolian = doomed to extinction

dodos = Cheerios; also called donut seeds

doe = female white-tailed deer or female snowshoe hare

dogmantick = "Guy loves da mutts, eh?"

dognuts = donuts

dog soup = water

dollar butt or dollar ass = Northern flicker. Name derives from silver-dollar-size white patch of feathers that can be seen when the bird flies away. Also sometimes called a yellow hammer in far western U.P. This nickname comes from the bird's many yellow feathers and its ability to loudly and rapidly hammer holes into tree bark.

doltage = old age

do-me-date = "Da sure t'ing, eh."

Dominiko nabisko = [Faux Latin] Da dead lingo; approximation for *Dominus vobiscum* [Latin], meaning "The Lord be with you."

donkey britches = Donkey bridges; meaning clumsy segues from one topic to the next, as in "Youse want eat deer meat, and how dat muffler workin' on da camp truck?"

donkey-tonk = honky-tonk

don't-cares = not interested

doo = too; or a womyn's new 'airstyle

doodilly = This term for a Manhattan is seemingly indigenous to mid-Menominee County.

dooley = any large pickup truck

door-wall, da = sliding-glass door; patio door

dope operas = also da soap sloperas

dopes' meds = home remedies

dose = those

dotstop = period at end of a sentence

double-aught buckshot = "Dose small, marble-size steel ball bearings [actual size: 00] loaded into shotgun shell which will de-limb and de-leaf ever't'ing 'tween shooter an' deer/bear/moose, an' a great chunk a da critter, too."

double loser = paranoid; "Don't trust sef, nor nobody else neder-eder."

downered = surprised, disrupted

downside-up = upside-down

downstate = anywhere Below the Bridge and south of the U.P. (synonym for BTB)

downwrite = write down; make a note

dozenmacallits or dozt'ingies = Any sort of product normally sold by the dozen, like roses and other flowers, eggs, beer, crawlers (earthworms for da baits), and often small traps for fur harvesters.

drain-freeze = frozen pipes

dreamocracy = democracy

dreck = wreck

dress-up band = symphony orchestra

drift = a pile of snow made by the wind, or a mine tunnel

dripple drops = stuff comes in dribs and drabs; little bits; also called drivelploops

drippydrabs = drips and drags

dripwood = driftwood

dronefly = "Gov'mint spy gizzies [gizmos] smaller'n agent's pinkynail."

droolery = psych or mental health facility

dross = "What da wymyns wears."

drumbambambeatabangatree = jamboree

drumble = move slowly, sluggishly

drumlin = a small, glacially created bump of land

Drummond, or D.I. = Drummond Island, at eastern tip of the U.P., accessible by car ferry from village of Detour on the peninsular mainland.

drunting = hunting while legally intoxicated; illegal, and heavily punished (when caught)

dryasdust = boring

dryquicksand = fine-grained sugar sand; "Can swallow youse's truck."

duck-dive = to flee, elude

ducks in da lineup, put allda = have all your ducks in a row

duck test = "If look like da duck and sound like da duck . . ."

duddyfunk = venison pie

Dullocramps = Democrats

dullpool = roomful of dumbasses

dumbicle = imbecile; "Can't hep been born dat way, eh."

dump duck = bald eagle; "Dey hangin' 'round da dumps allatime." Also known as snowheads.

dumperoo = to jilt, dump

E

'ead = head

earcheck = hearing check

earhats = ear muffs

easypee = extrasensory perception (ESP); "Youse know, read da udder guy's mind."

eataceous = gluttonous; extreme hunger

eatcelery = et cetera

Eater Bunny = "Dey make 'em outen chocolate at Eatertime."

eatibles = edibles

eats'itology = "Study at codges 'bout different s'it."

ecofreakos or eekyfreakies = people who consider ecology a form of theology

eder = either

eekreeple = weird, scary

eggnergy = energy

eh = All-purpose word used to end sentences, whether a question mark is implied or not. [Author's note: Rough equivalent of the modern use of "so" or "like" to begin sentences, serving as a conjunctive connector. This sound/word/expression in some areas of the U.P. may more often be *hey*, rather than *eh*, but with the same function and purpose. *Eh* can be a verbal period, an exclamation point, or a comma, eh. Or it can just be habit, put dat in at da end, eh. Like starting sentences, with "so." It has only recently dawned on me that perhaps the ubiquity of eh-use may be an attempt to tack on the Finnish word for no (*Ei* = no), as a means of seeking agreement with the statement just made, eh? (No?)]

Ei = [Finnish] No (pronounced *Ay!* and thus, not so different from *eh*). [Author's note: Be careful to catch context in Yooper talk, so as not to confuse with *Ei*, eh?]

elecrecruited = electrocuted

electaroll codge = Electoral College

electropoop = electropop (musical genre)

ELF line = ELF stands for Extra Low Frequency, which was a means used to communicate with submerged submarines on nuclear patrol around the world. These antennae used huge ground rock formations to serve as transmitters, and one such was located in Dickinson County. There was a lot of controversy over its potential effect—mainly on wildlife, not so much human health. Upshot: Hunters put their blinds along the ELF line and used the area to ambush deer and bear.

elk = Moose, sort of, in some places. [Author's note: Wapiti is elk here in the United States, but the word *elk* in Scandinavia means our moose, and therefore, their elk are our moose. "Our" wapiti are not indigenous to other parts of the world, apart from a few ranges in western Canada. Got it?]

emmet = any

Empster's Dumpingstar = Dempster's Dumpster; a common term for a specific brand of trash bins. (The actual major products for waste-handling trucks were called the Dempster Dumpmaster and the Dempster Dinosaur.)

encrypt = "Da dit-dot an' click-clack or somepin' do wit' da graves."

endlong = lengthwise

endolphins = endorphins

enema = enemy

enew = dive right in

'Enry = Henry Ford. The great entrepreneur spent a lot of time in the U.P. and employed a lot of people, who respected him without understanding (or caring about) his politics. He also raised the daily factory wage to $5 in Dearborn during the great mine strike in the Keweenaw (in 1913), thus motivating heaps of miners to immediately quit and beat it south to Detroit for more money and considerably safer jobs.

enveloper = (land) developer

equalatazor = equator; "Ha'f da way fum somewheres."

'er, er = her; and sometimes, "or" [Author's note: Never understood why, but Yoopers seem to insist on applying gender tags to virtually everything. When they can't figure out if it's an it or a he or a she, they seem to lean heavily toward the feminine "she." Which means in this age of newly emerging gender pronouns, things up north may get very interesting, and perhaps even instructive.]

erection = election

erotic = exotic

'ers = hers

escapegoat = scapegoat

Esky = Escanaba

espickdickgustly = expeditiously

etch or etches = edge or edges

Ethelbrad = "Jus' some demm Biking [Viking]."

ethnishitty = ethnicity

eunich = unique

eunichy = unity

ev't'ing = everything

Ex-Laxidaisycall = lackadaisical

explorator = explorer

extreme weather event = Yoopers and others who live in extreme
snow country don't get overly excited by blizzard warnings and
such. Here is an alleged actual Daily Weather Bulletin report from
North Dakota from October 2005. It could have been issued anywhere from Idaho to Maine. This October 28, 2005, bulletin came
from the emergency manager of Eddy County in North Dakota
concerning the winter storms that hit North Dakota October 4–5,
2005. Please note the many truths in the description of events.

> WEATHER BULLETIN: Up here in the Northern Plains, we
> just recovered from a Historic—may I even say "Weather Event
> of Biblical Proportions"? With a historic blizzard of up to 24
> inches of snow and winds to 50 mph, which broke trees in half,
> stranded hundreds of motorists in lethal snowbanks, closed all
> roads, isolated scores of communities, and cut power to tens of
> thousands. George Bush did not come . . . FEMA staged nothing
> . . . no one howled for the government . . . no one even uttered
> an expletive on TV . . . nobody demanded $2,000 debit cards .
> . . no one asked for a FEMA trailer house . . . no news anchors
> moved in. We just melted snow for water, sent out caravans to
> pluck people out of engulfed cars, fired up woodstoves, broke
> out coal-oil lanterns (Aladdin lamps), and put on an extra layer of
> clothes. Even though a Category 5 blizzard of this scale has never
> fallen this early . . . we know it can happen and how to deal with
> it ourselves. Everybody is fine."

[Author's note: This report could just as easily have come out of the
U.P. Limpy would be quick to tell youse, "Pipples up 'ere in 'mer-
gencies look ta each other, not ta da demm gov'mint.]

eye-boil = sty

eyegirlie = female optometrist/optician

eye-in-da-woods = trail-cam or game-camera

eyeland = optometrist or optician's office

eyeman = male optometrist/optician

Eyerack = Iraq

Eyeran = Iran

eyes = Walleyes; member of the perch family. Very tasty sweetwater fish. When spawning takes place in early spring, restaurant prices of walleye tend to drop along the Lake Michigan coast down to Chicago, as the fish markets flood with illegally taken fish. Spring fish runs are very busy times for fish cops; *see also* "conservation officer."

F

face hat = hide emotions, never show feelings

faceplant = either to fall flat on your face, or to be knocked down face-first

fair chase = "Dis a choke sign dey put up on dose hunt ranches where pay big money kill wall-hangers. *Fair chase* mean got walk fifty-yard from tower blind wit' soft chair ta deer, have pitcher made, an' okay dere, sport, dat be ten t'ousan'd bucks, dude. Da client jamokes wit' da money is killers, not no hunters. Ha ha, joke's on dem!"

Fairy's wheel = Ferris wheel

faith bender = jamoke drunk on churchy Kool-Aid

Fakesbook or Basebook = Facebook

fakes of fortune = fates of fortune

fackry = factory

fally = folly

Falsies Baregear = Folies Bergère; "Over to da Frockland [France]"

fambly = family

fambly valveyous = family values

farking = fucking

far-lookers = binoculars

far-talker = telephone

fartate = to let out a fart

farteur = (from lopsided Yooper French) gas artist

fartsack = sleeping bag

far-writer = telegraph; "Youse 'member, dat t'ing go tippy tap-tap all way crosst ocean way backety when."

fast-fix = jury-rigged

fastinate = hurry up; move it

fast-moving poop, da = diarrhea; *see also* "collywobbles"

fats = deep-dwelling lake trout; also called water skunk; "Dey taste like youse know what, eh?"

fat tax = flat tax; "T'ing would he'p dose guys already got heap more, get more heap."

faulterize = to fix blame

favit = favorite

fearfulsomeness = to be afraid

Febawary = February

feedy = ate too much

feets–paddle = skateboard

fenced meat = animals trapped inside trophy-game ranch fences

fender food = "Dis deer youse might hittin' wit' youse's truck," or can also refer to a friend-or-foe situation. Yooper violators have been known to run down game wardens and competitors.

fender-leaner = flagman on highway crew

ferret, go = (verb) like a bloodhound, nose around, see what you can find

fibricate = tell tad bituva lie; a small one, whitish lie

FIBTAB = Common Yooper anti-tourist term: Fricking Illinois Bastards Towing a Boat.

fidgy = get antsy, nervous, fidgety

Fiffmintmint = Fifth Amendment. "Dat t'ing where youse don't gotta answer cops or da prostituter 'cause youse know youse're guilty, so youse don't say nuttin', which is same sayin' youse guilty."

figgumate = fire-spitter

fingerbird, da = midpoint; or flashing the middle digit

finger claws = fingernails; *see also* "toe claws"

fingernailer = cliff-hanger

finger of speech = figure of speech

finger-pull, da (Granpa's fart gun) = Da fake fart gun ta make kittles laugh (a fatherly and grandfatherly specialty).

finickicity = picky, whiny, particular, fussy

Finlandia = Finlandia University, in Hancock, over channel from Houghton, formerly Suomi College

Finnana = Finnish banana; toast made from sliced hot-dog buns

Finndians = Finns married to Indians

Finnlander = anyone of Finnish descent

Finnlander formalwear = clean sweatshirt; super fancy requires a hoodie

Finnlander shish kebab = flaming arrow through a garbage-can lid

firefly = lightning bug

first ice, last ice = "Dese da two bes' times for fishin'; also da two bes' times for gettin' drownded."

fish car = "An old veek [vehicle] filled with youse's fishin' gear, loaded, gassed up, and ready to go on a moment's notice."

fish cop or fish pig = *see* "conservation officer"

fish house = commercial fish buyer/seller

fish snake = eel

five-scar = five-star; "Da best, eh."

fizzgig = a tease; also, skirty-flirty (or shirty-flirty, if it's a guy)

fizzygiggles/floozygigs = da skirty-flirty wymyns

flaggies = "Dose jamokes dat wave flag alla time at ev't'ing, an' mosta dose jamokes never worn no uniform."

flame = fame

flatlander = A mildly derogatory term for anyone from BTB, though there are lots of flat areas in the U.P.

flavorite = favorite

flense = to skin an animal

flightseeing = airborne tuursts; "Dose jamokes fum BTB like go airplane, here-dere-all-over place, see sights."

flimmy-flam = to cheat; dissemble

flip-flop nation = "Pipples don't know how ta wear real kicks no more. Dey wear dose t'ings in winner, wah!"

flittermouse = a bat

flivver = An old Ford model, but term sometimes applied to any old vehicle whose identity is not immediately known. It's also the nickname of Kingsford High School sports teams.

floccit = worthless

flockin' tree = roost, as with turkeys, turkey vultures, or crows

floordrobe = clothes strewn all over

floorsight = foresight

flopside = flipside

flusherushergusher = toilet

flushgush, da = indoor plumbing

flutterby = butterfly; "Which ain't no fly, an' ain't got no butter in it, eh."

fly = common housefly, or "Dat feather-fur stuff made by da ol' flyfloggers."

flyblown = maggoty

fly-flogger = fly-fisher

Flying Air Castle = Unidentified Flying Object (UFO) or Unidentified Aerial Phenomena (UAP); or Completely Ridiculous Alien Piffle (CRAP), the term Limpy prefers. "Onny bonkers pipples belee' dat crap, eh?"

flying rat or flying hog = seagull, or any loud, voracious seabird hanging around ports or towns

fly sweater = fly swatter

FMBM = For Me, By Me; a sort of personal version of "America First"

fodder or fadder = father

fogeyate = old, worn-out, outdated; "Dat ol' fart wear dat fogeyate chirt forty year!"

fogrizzle = a mix of foggy and drizzly

folder = quitter; no guts, no *sisu*

fool's gold = diff'ent t'ings for diff'ent pipples

football = American football; feetsball is soccer. "Use bot' dere feets ta move da ball."

footle = a time-waster

footlifting = Yooper fuel economy technique, hold foot off gas whilst descending hills.

forda = for the

forenoon = morning

forkersnorks or fortersnorts = fisherman's forceps; "When find 'em dere at bottom of back pocket in da fish vest, under all youse's crap, youse laff, make da big snort. *Dere* youse buggers are!"

forkhorn = Usually a young deer with an antler on each side that looks like a "Y."

fornaccolite = An acolyte in a certain life-sustaining activity; "Jus' learnin' how ta do da youse- know-what . . ."

Forty-Niner = Ostensibly this is a Native American dance, but in powwow circles it refers to stepping away to a "secretly" staged post-party held somewhere near the powwow, but the location is *not* disclosed to Tribal leaders and adults, etc. According to one origin story, a group of Native American youths wanted to enter a sideshow—billed as either "Days of Forty-Nine" or "Girls of Forty-Nine"—at the Caddo County Fair in Anadarko, Oklahoma (the center of the Kiowa and Comanche populations circa mid-nineteenth century). When they couldn't come up with the price of admission, one young man reportedly said, "Let's have our own forty-nine," and so the dance, in this version, acquired its own name. Another version of the name's etymology dates its use to 1924, when the movie *In the Days of '49* was particularly popular in the Anadarko area. A separate origin story presents the name "forty-nine dance" as a commemorative reference to a group of fifty warriors who went to battle, with only forty-nine returning, or, conversely, with only one returning and forty-nine killed. Who knows what the real facts or truth are; forty-ninin' means "Let's party, dudes!"

F.O.T. = fuck-off time; flex time; "Tell boss youse's workin' when youse's oota camp."

fouddroy = a dazzler

four-hooves north = dead

4WD = four-wheel drive; a must for all Yooper vehicles, especially in winter, or off-road conditions

four-wheeler = ATV with four wheels; small veek designed to go off-road

fowling piece = big-gauge (8-gauge, 10-gauge, etc.), long-barreled shotgun

frankenstink = a stench; odiferous

fredora = fedora; "Kind hat eder da wymyns or da mens can wear."

freeball = no skivvies

freeskate = cheapskate

freezefryer = cryogenic tank

frightled = scared, spooked

fritch or lecktrickedified icybox, da = refrigerator (fridge)

frock = frog

Frockland or Frockyland = Frogland (France)

frocknostigate = prognosticate; "Guess da future."

frog t'roat = froggy throat; laryngitis

frosty = not happy, pissed off, irritated

F.U. = initials of Finlandia University in Hancock; home of the Finlandia Lions

fuckit list = "Da shit youse ain't never gone do."

fuderunt = (pronounced *FOOD-er-unt*) Someone boisterous, loudly obnoxious; long ago, this word was derived from *foudroyant*, meaning "sudden and overwhelming in effect."

fudgie = A tourist on Mackinac Island; by the way, Mackinac Island, though north of the Lower Peninsula, is *not* considered by many (or maybe most) Yoopers to be part of the Yoop. Not sure what the islanders think, or if they even care.

fuhgit = forget

fum = from

FUMTU = Fucked Up More Than Usual; used most often by non-vets.

furgood = frigid; "Youse know, when da wedder, she go really cold, dat's when youse wears da furs, make youse feel good."

G

gabble-gobble = trash talk

gabbyquacious = a nonstop, empty-headed talker

Gaddisfly = Caddis fly

gagitous = "Somepin' so stinky make youse want hurl."

Galiporny = "Where go all da hot-body girlies ta make porn films."

galleytosis = A terrible, cloying smell in the kitchen; or halitosis (bad breath, which is a Madison Avenue / advertising term, not the scientific name for a medical condition).

gallopsy = always in a hurry, and somewhat clumsy and reckless

gallowsbird = raven

Galzheimers = "When forget names of da wymyns youse usta see."

gameoflesh or camelflesh = camouflage

game warden = *see* "conservation officer"

gandermooner = "Hugbies who stray during wifey's monthly."

gangstapruner = entrepreneur

gapeseed = anyone or anything that attracts unwanted attention, like from cops

Garden, da = The Garden Peninsula hangs down into northern Lake Michigan, between Manistique and Rapid River. Site of many violent confrontations between conservation officers and commercial fish violators. Still considered by law enforcement to be a lawless place.

gas = glass

GASCAR = NASCAR

gasdestroid = asteroid

Gaseous Clay = Cassius Clay; "Dat Muhammer Ali guy, da scrapper."

gash money = cash money

gashole = environmentalist

gasino = casino

gas laugh = horselaugh

gas roots = grassroots

gasserole = casserole; also called widower dish

gatherling place = *see* "tavern"

gazinta = goes into

Gazpacho = Gestapo [Author's note: Limpy heard this on the idiot box from some wingnut congresswoman from out west, and he's been saying it ever since.]

Geck! = sound of disgust

Gee-Are = GR (Grand Rapids)

geezer house = any nursing home, retirement home, or assisted living facility

geezhund = "Old guy runs around wit' da wymyns 'alf 'is age."

Geez-O-Pete = mild exclamation of frustration; occasionally it's a borderline invective

Gemütlichkeit = [German] "Mean da good times an' warm feelings. Dose ol' Chermans in da taverns like talk dis."

genitals = generals; "Dem a beek dogs give da orders."

gentarch = male head of the family

George = the late governor, George Romney

George it! = Old game warden term for charging into a situation with minimal caution, planning, or forethought.

getbacks, da = interest earned on an investment; or revenge

get-some words = sweet nothings

ghetto gas = blues and jazz music

ghost slappers = flip-flops

ghost trees = sycamores

gibbershite = meaningless drivel

Gibby = Kirk Gibson, Michigan State and Tigers star; not a Yooper, but his performance and character rate first-name fame among Yooper Tigers fans.

giffgaff = give-and-take

giggolodatchit = look it up; google-that-shit

gillygaloo = Oddball, something out of place, foreign, doesn't fit; the name for a mythical bird that lays square eggs.

gintonic = genetic

Gitche Gumee = Lake Superior to the Ojibwa

gitways = hidden trails; evasion routes

give or bake = give or take

givin 'er = Going all in and all out; giving the full effort you're capable of—akin to leaving it all on the field. The opposite of going through the motions. When a Yooper says, "I'm givin' 'er," they're at max effort.

gleeter = trickster, phony, cheater, liar, thief

glidgy = squinty

gloomonta = grab hold and don't let go

G'Lordygasm! = orgasm

glory story = obituary; also deadswords

glusk = loaf; duck work

glustery = combo of gusty and blustery

gnashjaw = "Standin' aroun' an' sayin' nuttin'."

goat = coat

goat rodeo or group grope = a disorganized group effort turned disaster goatsmeal = oatmeal

goatstown = ghost town; "All youse see is goats eatin' grass offen da old streets."

gobbeldeygab = any foreign language

gofastslow, da = "Put 'er goin' easy, keep 'er movin', don't do nuttin' stoopid draw 'tention to seff."

go finger = go figure

Gogebic County = (pronounced *Go-GIB-ic*, or sometimes *Go-GIP-ic*) "Youse know, over dere wit' da Stormy Kromer fackry in Bez'mer."

Go-Gookle dat shit! = Google it!

goitering = loitering

golden surp = golden syrup (i.e., molasses, corn syrup, etc.)

goldwifeystail = old wives' tale

gone = going to; went

gone Wartholean = get all heady and snooty over temporary claim to fame

gonnery sack = gunnysack; "Put da dead stuff in 'em."

gonunda = gone under, deceased, dead

Good greek! = Good grief!

Gookle = Google

go Putin = "Dat Russky jamoke runs 'roun' wit' 'is chirt offen."

Gordie = Late Hall of Famer Gordie Howe, No. 9—one of the greatest hockey players ever.

gorilla in da rain = gorilla in the room; unspoken, unidentified influence

gorty = bad-tempered, nasty disposition

"Got a question for youse" = This is by far the most frequent approach citizens use to greet conservation officers.

go Tarzan = turn wildman

got go gym = Limpyism (not Yooper-wide); "I need to use the restroom."

got-go-roundybounce = traffic roundabout; "Some pipples get goin', just keep bounce 'round da circle, can't figger how heck to get out! Lights was better."

Gott = God

gotta = got to; sometimes go-do

Gottauditory = God's voice

Gott's Country = What Yoopers call the U.P., especially those who move away in order to make a living and miss it while they are gone. Many of these folks tend to retire back to the Yoop when their work lives are done. The place has that kind of a powerful hold on people's imaginations and hearts.

Gott's palm = psalm

Gott's past = "Da one don't never change, eh."

Gottsweed = Indian sweetgrass; for smudging during religious ceremonies, not for smoking

go Twinkie = Means to go postal, wig out, run amok; "Den youse blame t'ing on 'count youse got da sweetbloods [diabetes] an' youse 'ad too much sugar an' dat was all she wrote, see? Was da fault ovda Twinkie, not youse's. Claim dis as defense, see how she goes. Won't be first time dis been tried." [Author's note: Once upon a time in some places it was not considered a crime to kill someone whilst under the influence, the substance being the source of blame, not the killer.)

gourmaggot = gourmet

gov'mint = government

grainitude = gratitude

gralloch or lights = guts, innards

grandee = big shot

grape (Mad Dog) MD 20/20 = Yooper champagne

grassant = croissant; "One dose fancy Frock [French] bak'ry t'ings, no holes."

grass-eater or grassivorous = vegetarian

grass snake = garter snake

gravidude = "Stone-cold in 'is heart"; deadly, dangerous

gravity-pee, da = outhouse

gray jay or Canada jay or camp robber or whiskey jack = (*Perisoreus canadensis*) Ornithologists called these birds Canada jays until 1957, when the official name became gray jay, but many Yoopers prefer to use their more colorful tags of camp robbers or whiskey jacks.

Gray Lady, Da = Lake Superior

grayslick = calm water before a bad storm

grayzone, da = right–wrong spectrum

Great-Big-Gott-Box-a-Cash = megachurch

greendream = euthanasia; "Vet puts down da pets an' 'urt critters dis way."

greenstone = State gemstone found in the Keweenaw Peninsula and on Isle Royale. Polished and made into jewelry, often in combination with native pink gold from Ropes Gold Mine near Ishpeming.

Gretchen = Michigan governor Gretchen Whitmer, who was vehemently and often criticized by Donald Trump from the White House. She roundly ignored him, and remains much maligned by some Yooper Trumpers.

griefers = grieving, sad people

griller = gorilla

grills = grilse (young salmon); "Sometimes can mean da young wymyns too."

groan = groin

grockery or grossery = grocery, depending on the cleanliness of the store

grocks = groceries

groggery = booze; liquor store

groggleyed = goggle-eyed

groin = groan

grout = gout

grow da tail = defecate; take a dump

growlflusters = "Way pipples get when somebody lose temper an' ev't'ing get messy."

grrrin = combination grin and snarl

grubble = rubble; "Like all dat stuff piles up onda bottom of river."

gruffledy = angry, perturbed

grumplestrips = "Dose raised-up t'ings on da highways he'p keep youse awake at night."

grumpoid = grumpy; ill-tempered

grutch, da = grudge; pronounced a lot like grudge (garage)

GTJ/GDJ = Gookle That/Dat Junk

guardoggian angle = guardian angel

guff = lip, crap, backtalk

gullimouche = a sap, a sucker; an easy target for grifters; gullible

Gulpamessico = Gulf of Mexico

gunboots = gumboots

gunk = any grease or mold

gunta or gone = Going to; Limpy prefers "gone," others, the other.

gusty = tasty, savory

gutbite = instinct

gutholed = hungry

guts-go = gusto

gwackamexamunchy goop = guacamole; "Cheesus, who eats dat goopy green-crap?'

gweet = go eat; "We gone gweet wingy Wents-day down to da VFW."

H

habitchulcated = habituated

hacktors = actors; also "fakers"

haffacaff = coffee mix, caffeine with decaf

hair-dry = air-dry

hairflynomic = "Guys wit' dat sweep-back hair allas look like da wind pick 'em up, make 'em fly away, eh?"

hairloon = heirloom; "Dat olden crap an' stuff, eh?"

hairsafryin' = excited; hair-on-fire

hair toll = balding; the price of a long life

hairyassmint = harassment

Haitcheffie (HFE) = Horizontal Frictional Exercise; coitus; intercourse; sex

Halfrica = Africa

Halfrican = mixed race, black and white

halko = [Finnish] a log, three-feet-plus long (one meterish)

hallucajacentation = hallucination

Halverson bar = Henderson bar; thirty- to sixty-pound, four- to five-feet-long, straight, heavy steel bar with wedge edge, used to pry things, dig holes, crack and smash rocks, or bash just about anything needing bashing. Highly useful tool. [Author's note: Can be a great equalizer in a bar fight—*if* you're strong enough to wield the thing.]

hambone burial = "Youse buy da cheap hambone at Pat's or Larry's or Econofoods, or Jack's or Gary's. Stick dat bone up da dearly departed's butt, dump 'im oot in da woods for da wolfies an' udders to tek da care of. Cost almost nuttin', an' ought mebbe make good day for da critters, eh?"

hammer-handle = Northern pike; a fish of many moods, with many, many, very sharp teeth.

H'ammerzon = Amazon; "Dose guys, dey beatin' hell outen ev'body in biz."

H'Anatomony H'Awards = Academy Awards, "for best wymyns bods, eh?"

handacossda = accost

hand-brain = da TV remote control

hang-down, da = mullet haircut

hang genade = hand grenade

hanglecuffs = handcuffs

hangstring = hamstring

hanking = clawing and scratching

hanoi = annoy

hankycramped = handicapped; "Got somepin' goofy witchas, can't do ev't'ing like reg'lar pipples." [Author's note: Interestingly, while many Yoopers bemoan what they see as ludicrous rules, and sometimes complain about designated parking for the handicapped, they rarely encroach on such spaces, *even* in spaces in parking lots dozens of miles from civilization.]

Happy Rock = nickname for Gladstone, in Delta County, between Escanaba and Rapid River

hard-cooked cack = hard-boiled egg

hard tack = Biscuits made of water, flour, and salt; very long-lasting. *See also* "slumgullion."

hardtop = paved highway or street; also called blacktop

hard water = ice

h'army, da = the army

Harrison = The late Jim Harrison was a poet, novelist, writer, outdoorsman, gourmet, gourmand, and raconteur raised in Northern Michigan. He lived for many years in a farmhouse in Leelanau County (BTB); he also had a camp on the Blind Sucker River east of Grand Marais, in Northern Alger County. The U.P. featured in many of his stories, some of which were made into films. Ironically he was always more honored in France than in the United States.

h'assjunks = adjunct; "Extra parts for somepin' nobody want pay for."

Havedatumblie & Wench = Abercrombie & Fitch, sporting goods and outfitters

hayroll = outdoor sex

headaker = headache

headbobbers = "Dose jamokes, dere 'eads all over da place when talk, 'cause dey fulla da s'it."

headlighting = The employment of vehicle headlights to spot, freeze, and illegally shoot deer. Can recognize this by the S-pattern drivers sometimes follow as they drive the roads, swinging lights from one side to the other. [Author's note: If you shine a bright light in a deer's face and eyes, it will freeze momentarily, allowing the violator to shoot while the animal is frozen in place. Illegal to do this.]

headshaker = Someone whose behavior is so erratic or foolish it makes others just shake their heads.

headwaters = "Where t'ings start."

H'earfth = Earth

heart attack snow or mashed potato snow = Heavy, wet, gluey snow; difficult to lift or move with a shovel.

heavity, or gravy toss = seriousness; gravitas

heavy roads = impassable

Hebowler = Ebola

Heikki Lunta = [Finnish] imaginary Finnish god of snow and ice (winter)

Heittää löylyä? = [Finnish] "Okay I t'row more water on da rocks [in da sauna]?"

Hell = Anywhere that's not in the U.P.

hellamintree = elementary

hell-bat = bat out da hell

hellhole = Any city not in the U.P.

helltown headache = hangover

helluvablow = hullabaloo

hematite = a kind of iron ore

Hemingfake = Hemingway; *see* "Two-Hearted River"

Hemlock = Heimlich maneuver; "Way unchoke chokers, eh?"

hemmy-haw = hem and haw

hemocide = homicide

Henderson bar = Though this is technically the correct name, *see* "Halverson bar."

h'ep = help

herbies = herpes

heremute = A hermit who doesn't believe in anything or anyone, and refuses to talk.

heromoans or sheromoans = hormones; "Dose t'ings make youse t'ink youse some kinda Stuporman, by make youse t'ink youse can do stoopid t'ings. If womyn, dese t'ings called sheromoans."

Hetkinen = [Finnish] Just a minute.

Hex hatch = Annual middish-summer event when huge *Hexagenia limbata* flies pop out of mud banks (when mud reaches a certain temperature); huge fish gorge on these insects at all stages of development. Also called "Michigan Mayflies," "Fishflies," and other things. The largest brown trout of the year are often caught during this hatch, which is largely a nocturnal event.

hey = synonym/surrogate for "eh"

hibby-jibby = close call

hickabilly = country music

hickeyups = hiccups

hides 'is light under da brothel = hides his light under a bushel

high-heather = high spirits

highpusscrissy = hypocrisy

high-speed beef = white-tailed deer

hightailer = chipmunk; also called squeakmunk

hippedy-dippedy = hippie

hippie-commie-red libtard = Anyone who doesn't vote Repub-
licramp or spout Republican Party line, or votes for, or even
considers voting for, or even says anything slightly favorable to, the
Democramps/Democraps.

hippodermic = hypodermic needle; "Youse see how *big* some dose
needles? Wah!"

hippygrift = hypocrite

hirvio = [Finnish] moose-thingy; a monster; something big and
imposing

Hispaniard = Hispanic

hi-speed-wireless-device = any firearm, especially a handgun

histiprickles = porcupines

historyechtomy = no sense whatsoever of the past

hobo = oboe

hobsnob = hobnob

hockey kick = "Knock down jamoke by tap da heel uvda foot wit'
weight on 'er as 'e moves, an' down 'e goes, eh?" Also called
heel kick.

hog strips = bacon

hokeymus pokeymus = hocus pocus, magic, trickery

holes-in-a-bowl = colander

Holy Wah! = Equivalent of *Luffda!* [Swedish] or "Holy shit!" Sometimes shortened to Wah!

homelanding = homeland

HOMES = Easy way to remember the five Great Lakes: **H**uron-**O**ntario-**M**ichigan-**E**rie-**S**uperior.

homophones = "Da ones dose gay guys call each udder wit'?"

honey = money

honeyfudger = Someone who always makes things out to be sweeter than they are.

hong = hog

Hong Kong = King Kong, and vicey versa

honk = "Ta blow youse's beak real loud."

honking = Engaging in very loud, strenuous, and energetic sex.

Honolulu Blue = Unique blue color created for Detroit Lions football, used only by the club in their materials and team uniforms.

hooch = any and all alcoholic beverages

hooey-buoy = hyperbole

hoof it or hump it = To go on foot, walk fast; can also mean make a decision: go, or no go?

hooker, line, and stinker = hook, line, and sinker

hookertute = prostitute

hooking = Also called bum-riding, skitching, shacking, or shagging. A means of winter travel where pedestrians grab onto the back bumper of a truck or auto, squat down, and ski/skate down a snow- or ice-covered road on their boot/shoe soles. [Author's note: Trust me on this; a patch of bare pavement can seriously spoil the ride.]

hooleygums = hooligans; "Da gott-demm Irish Micks, dose guys talk da big game, like talk wit' dere dukes an' wit' dere words. Got beat 'em up ta shut 'em up."

Hoover = any vacuum cleaner; to vacuum

hopelescent = Can mean somebody afraid to hope; or, "So much hope, dere skin's all lightered up."

hork = cough or hock, as in hocking up a loogie (or "lungey")

hornage or ornch = orange

hornia = hernia

horneymoon = honeymoon

hornswindle = cheat, mislead, deceive

horserumpyrunt = a jockey

horse sweat = lather; or cheap liquor

HO-ton = Houghton, in where else—Houghton County

Hottywood = Hollywood

houndsmen = Hunters who at certain times of the year, in certain places, can use dogs to legally pursue and take game.

House of Ill Dispute, or Villa Gonorrhea = Da Clap House

House of Losers or Graybar Hotel = jail, prison

how–far, da = range-finding scope; range-finder

how–long, da = ruler or yardstick

howver = however

hugamanganamus = humongous

hugby = hubby; husband

huivi = [Finnish] (pronounced *wee-vee*) A huge head scarf that covers even the mouth, worn in snow season, "especially inna storm when youse's oot blowin' da white dirt ooten da driveway."

Hukassa = [Finnish] Means "in a wolf," which translates to "You're lost!"

hull = whole; all

hull boot an' kabibble = everything; the whole kit and kaboodle

hull honk = whole hog

humanatorium = "Where dump ol' fritches."

humbunk = humbug

humdinger = exemplary; "A real beaut!"

hump = To go on foot, or a slight bump in the ground. (In Vietnam the term *hump* was commonly used for foot travel, and usually meant moving with some dispatch over a fair distance.)

hungry dory = hunky dory

Hunters' Ball = A common bar promotion angle during firearm deer season.

Hunters' Supper = "Open-to-da-public (for da fee), dese suppers put on by da surface [service] clubs an' church groups, usually night before the opener."

hunter's white = Color of hunting clothes often employed during the so-called "late" muzzleloader and bow seasons for deer, in December. This is after the heavy white-dirt winter blanket has settled in and is piling up. [Author's note: Not to be confused with a "white hunter."]

huntin' camp widows = "Youse see, huntin' camp's mostly for da mens . . . so when wifeys or hugbies go oot ta camp, some uvda udder hugbies/wifeys sometimes go bars look for da good times (foolin' aroun' an' such, ya know?)." We know, Limpy, we know.

hurl = vomit

husk = tusk

hyperdolt = dumb as a bolt; really stupid, lacking in intelligence

hypermimer = talks sign language real fast

hyperpoop = overrated; baloney; grift

hypothermia = Gradual or fast loss of core body heat can lead rapidly to the shakes, shock, and death. When someone starts to get the shakes, get them to warmth immediately. This condition happens most when temperatures are in the 30s Fahrenheit, especially when it is raining or damp, and there is wet snow.

I

Ians, da = Immigrants from Slavic and central European countries that end with letters "ia" (e.g., Serbia/Serbians, Croatia/Croatians, Romania/Romanians, Bulgaria/Bulgarians, Russia/Russians, etc.).

ice dam = When anchor ice piles up, usually during spring melt or ice-out period, and breaks loose, floats downstream, hits obstacles, and piles up to block rivers or streams.

ice fog = Introduce a source of high heat to extreme cold, subzero temps (say, a jet engine), and the heat can create a *thick* fog that often has to be physically broken up—or it will just hang in place.

ice 'ockey = ice hockey; "Dis is game wit' mostly buncha white guys smackin' 'round frozed-up rubber disk look like da Moon Pie. P'ofessional 'ockey start up dere in Copper Country, not up Canuckland. (Prolly she invent by da Dutchmens, not dose Canucks or da Yoopers.)"

ice shanty = Temporary ice-fishing structure/shelter; some are very fancy and comfy inside.

ice spiders = Formations in newly formed ice, probably from ice bubbles; at first glance, this phenomenon looks like spiders. Seems to happen pretty much early and late in ice seasons.

Ichneumon (also called stump humpers or stump stabbers) = This species of wasp looks both intimidating and downright mean—like some creepy bioengineered super stinging beast, they are ovipositors, and use their long pokey things to insert their eggs into nests and larvae of other insects.

Ichneutic = This word has something to do with tracking or trailing someone or something. [Author's note: Which sort of fits with Yoopers and their hunting, fishing, and game wardens and all that, so we chucked 'er into the stew.]

ickmoronics = economics

ideal = idea

idiotball = basketball

If it flies, it dies = Unscrupulous waterfowl hunters who don't (or won't) take the time to actually identify different ducks, so they just attempt to kill all that come into their shooting range.

If it's red, it's dead = A poacher saying regarding deer hunting after July 4—after all deer coats have gone from their winter gray to sweet summer red. Meat is tastiest when fur is red.

If I were you, me = If I were you

Iggy = Nickname for St. Ignace (Mackinac County); local high school is LaSalle, home uvda St. Ignace LaSalle High School Saints.

ignoranus = ignoramus

Ike = IQ

Ikedaho = Idaho

Iketalian or Woptalian = Italian

Iketalian part'ritch = any crow or raven

illegal = sick bird

illegals = Yooper joke for Wisconsinites who hunt, fish, and trap more in the U.P. than in Wisconsin.

Illinoid = resident of Illinois

'im = him

IM = Iron Mountain in Dickinson County

imperial bull = A bull elk (wapiti) with seven points on each antler.

Imunna = I'm going to

inbreasts = breast implants

inbreathe = inhale

inby = inside, beside

Indi'n = Indian, the word neither racist nor pejorative, e.g., Keweenaw Bay Indian Community.

Indi'n bread = Frybread, similar to elephant ears; not cornbread, which is a common misconception.

inflammation = information

inkduress = interest (financially)

ink pencil = pen

inmanimal = inanimate

inna = in a

innasscate = interstate

innawoods = in da woods

Interweb = Internet

in velvet = A male deer regrows antlers annually. First growth is from spring to when preparation for fall rut commences, when the antlers are covered with fuzzy, mossy-looking substance filled with blood vessels. Bucks rub off this material in preparation for the rutting/mating (competition) season. "Dat velvet s'it stink *real* bad."

'ippers or 'ipboots = hipboots

IR = Iron River in Iron County

Irish confetti = bricks

iron sight = Old-fashioned sighting mechanism for rifles and rifled shotguns (vs. scopes, laser sights, etc.).

iron tonic = ironic

'is = his

Isle Royale = Island between Keweenaw Peninsula and Ontario in northern Lake Superior. Home to a beautiful and not easily reachable US national park and a more-than-half-century study of the relationship between wolves and moose and other prey.

'it = hit

ivry = ivory

ivrysnowland = "Places wit' white pipples onny."

IW = Ironwood in Gogebic County

Izzone = That part of the seating at Spartan basketball games populated by Spartan students, and honoring longtime MSU coach, Tommy Izzo of Iron Mountain.

J

jääkääppi = [Finnish] ice closet (refrigerator)

jabbawinkwinkedy = imaginary creature

jack = lumberjack or logger

jacklighting = Using artificial light to temporarily freeze deer in their tracks at night and shoot them. Also called shining and headlighting (the latter using car headlights rather than another artificial light to illuminate the deer). Definitely illegal if there is a weapon inside the vehicle, especially uncased and loaded . . .

jackpine savage = Someone who lives in the woods, often off the grid.

jack-pot = Contemptuous expression for an unskillful logging job. Also refers to more than one tree hanging up when another is felled.

Jacktown = Slang for Michigan State Prison in Jackson, Michigan.

Jaggate = A Lake Superior agate with natural markings that look like Mick Jagger's fat lips.

Jake = Dominic J. Jacobetti, famous U.P. politician

jamdice = jaundice

jamoke = All-purpose word for stranger, outsider, jerk; anyone the speaker looks down on

Jan'wary = January

jarbird = nuthatch

jargoggle = to befuddle

jark = to fake physically, to dodge; similar to jinking

jawsuit = lawsuit

jeepers = BTB jamokes come ATB (Above the Bridge), drive dere Jeeps an' mudders all over da place, don't care where.

Jeet, or Jeetyet? = Did you eat, or Did you eat yet?—as in, have you eaten? Eating is a big deal in severe snow country, and it's also part of the culture to be hospitable to friends and strangers alike.

jeffegy = effigy

jelly belly = Bismarck pastry

Jenny = Former Michigan governor Jennifer Granholm; Michigan citizens often refer to governors by their first names or nicknames.

jewishrewdence = jurisprudence

jibby = opossum

jicklepickled = turned around, confused, disoriented

Jimmy, or Hoffa = James Hoffa, the disappeared Teamsters union president. Jimmy owned land and a camp in the western U.P. Some Yoopers swear that's where he's "sleeping."

jink-an'-jank = To fake, physically swerve, or jump away from potential collision, or to make it hard for someone to see who you are as you flee.

jobber's sun = The moon; derives from loggers working early and late, when the only light available was sometimes lunar.

jockstrapadition = juxtaposition

Joemack = Joseph S. Mack (1919–2005). Usually pronounced as a single word, Joe Mack was a Democratic member of the Michigan Senate, representing much of the Upper Peninsula from 1967 to 1990.

Joe No-Pack = "Too broke ta buy beer."

johnny cakes = toilet fresheners

jolly = how one gets after two shots

joom = hurry up; go faster; "Move it, move it, move it! Joom-joom-joom!"

jornada = Trapper term for one day's journey, with no stops or rests.

joten kuten = [Finnish] just about

juke, or jook = *see* "jark"

jukejeepsoup = jujitsu

jumbo = quart of beer

Jumbo River = scenic, good, skinny brook trout water

jump shooting or potholing = Moving cautiously toward ducks, whether in a boat or on foot in order to flush them up to get a shot.

junkal region = "Da mans' an womyns' stuff 'down dere'"; da nether parts.

junkball = jumpball; a toss-up, meaning a situation that can go either way—for you, or against you

jutch = judge

Jutch Lynch = "Fuhgit jutch, dis when pipples get pissed, hang youse's ass."

juustoleipa or *juustoa* = [Finnish] squeaky cheeses, sometimes called bread cheeses

K

Kai = [Finnish] Can I?

Kaikki manne mita tule lika pusa ka = [Finnish] What goes around, comes around.

kakkis = [Finnish] low-lifes

kalakukko = [Finnish] Fish pie; a sort of pastry form, made with thin rye crust in the shape of a moccasin (da shoe, not da snake).

kale = rabbit chow

Kaline = Al Kaline, the best Tiger ever, a Hall-of-Famer.

kalsarikannil = [Finnish] Getting drunk in your underwear. [Author's note: This is a legitimate term reflecting (apparently) a culturally indigenous practice, but as of this writing, I haven't seen any clubs formed around it, or Facebook pages, etc.]

ka'nunkles = knuckles

kapowsky = a din, loud noise, ruckus

Kaydeebee (KDB) = kick da bucket; die

keck = beer keg

keek = a spy

keester, da = backside; butt

kenless = clueless

kerf = a notch in something

Keweenaw, Da = Pronounced *KEY-win-aw*, although lifelong locals
are more likely to pronounce it *KEY-vin-aw*, and be advised: A lot
of old-timers (dose lazy galoots) drop offen da "aw" at end and
say *KEY-vin-ah*. The peninsula, which is about one hundred miles
west of Marquette, juts north seventy or so miles from Houghton–
Hancock up to Copper Harbor. The Keweenaw is then a peninsula offen a peninsula, see? [Author's note: The Keweenaw is part
of so-called Copper Country, which to confuse things even more,
geographically and geologically stretches all the way down the
Keweenaw, and sweeps from Houghton down to Ontonagon
County. There was copper mining all through this long strip.]

Keweenaw canary = goldfinch

K. I., or Sawyer, or Da Base = K. I. Sawyer Air Force Base, now de-
commissioned and mothballed, located near Gwinn in Marquette
County. If Da Base is said in Chippewa County, it more likely
refers to the now-mothballed Kincheloe AFB. Formerly Kinross
AFB, it's located near Rudyard in Chippewa County, and is now
home to a federal prison. Kinross Correctional Facility (KCF) originally opened in 1977 by utilizing converted US Air Force build-

ings for most of its major structures. The facility then relocated to the closed Hiawatha Correctional Facility (1989–2009) in October 2015. The eight Level II housing units can accommodate up to 1,280 prisoners. KCF also maintains a housing unit near the site of the former facility, housing 320 Level I prisoners. The fifty-acre, maximum-security prison has ten buildings. Other former USAF locations/installations in the U.P. included a Bomarc missile site at Raco (Brimley area, in the eastern U.P.) and a radar station on Mount Bohemia in the Keweenaw Peninsula.]

kibbling = bail money

kickass = significant, good, beautiful, decisive

kickin' = overdone; too much; extra spicy

kicks = shoes, footwear

Kiitos = [Finnish] Thank you.

killshot = A bullet or arrow that kills an animal.

killy = thin ice; prolly derived from old-timey lingo, "Dat t'in ice will kill youse."

kinda, or kinuh = kind of

kinds = Relatives by blood; hitch-up, or just because; "Dey all da same kind."

king salmon = *see* "Chinook"

Kingsford = Where wood for Ford Motor Company "woodies" was once milled; Kingsford is located next to Iron Mountain in south Dickinson County.

kinskins = relatives, family

Kippis! = [Finnish] Cheers!

kithhog = left-handed

kittles = children of all ages and genders

kitty letter = kitty litter

Ki-Yi! = quasi-snarky term for Indians

klapi = [Finnish] firewood piece smaller than a *halko*

Klondiak Island = Kodiak Island, aka, "Where da brown bears watch da pipples."

Klondiak moment = Kodak moment; something memorable, and worth an on-spot, at-the-moment photograph.

kloof = steep drop, not quite a cliff

klypahollic = kleptomaniac

Knee, Da = Shorthand for Menominee (Menominee County)

kneejerkies = "Pipples say stuff, act, don't t'ink first."

knickpick = to nitpick

knickwit = nitwit

Knights Kevlar = Knights Templar

knowbowl or t'inkbone, da = the brain

korpu = [Finnish] rock-hard cinnamon toast; *see* "Trenary Toast"

Koskenkorva = [Finnish] Some Finns insist this is *the* vodka in Finn-landerland; sometimes shortened to Kossu.

kype = Dramatically hooked bump on the tip of the bottom jawbone that male trout and salmon develop during fall mating season.

L

Labordrawer reliever = Labrador retriever; "Kinda dog goes gets game so's youse can rest."

laff test = a test for bullshit (veracity); "Can youse say dat wit'oot youse or me laffin'? If not, den it's bulls'it."

Lake Fantyhose = Lake Fanny Hooe, just outside Copper Harbor at the tip of the Keweenaw Peninsula

lake-polished = agate naturally smoothed by waves and lake motion

Laker = Lake Superior agate; also means a lake trout

Lake State = Lake Superior State University in Da Soo, home ta da Lakers

lamprey = A species of eel that breeds in rivers, matures, and swims out into the Great Lakes, where it grabs on to various fish such as trout and salmonids and holds on. They act like remora on sharks. Sometimes you'll catch fish with lamprey scars, or with the eels *still hanging on* to them. In many parts of the world, lampreys are eaten, and prized as a delicacy. This particular delicacy does not seem to have found purchase here yet.

land yacht = large pickup truck

langitudes = latitudes and longitudes; "Dey too hard keep straight in head."

L'Anse Vegas = Humorous, mildly derisive, and clever term for the Keweenaw Bay Indian Community's casino in Baraga, Michigan, which is not even in L'Anse, but five miles or so west, around the head of the bay on the other side of Keweenaw Bay.

Lao juice = rice wine liqueur

lapaleprosy = lap of luxury

larrykicks = knee-high moccasins

larwhump = to beat severely

Last Day of Kingdom's Rum = Last day of Kingdom Come

last willing tentsdiment = last will and testament

lats = slats; homemade skis

lavas = larvae

lawsmen = Any peace officer or cop; anyone, male or female, who wears a badge.

lay fever = "When go tavern, dis girlie given you dis look, like how's 'boot youse-me?"

laystil = lay still

LBJ or LGJ = Little Brown Job, or Little Gray Job; means any bird of that color that Limpy can't identify and doesn't want to disclose that he doesn't know. When he's grumpy he may say LBF or LGF . . .

leaf peeper = Tuursts who come to the U.P. from all over the United States to view the fall color show, which in most years can be astonishing.

learn me = teach me

Leaverdere = Leave it/her there.

Leaverite = Word used by experienced rock hunters for amateurs; "Leaverite dere where youse finded 'er." Translation: The stone is worthless, except perhaps to you.

lebanese = lesbian

'lecktrick steps = escalator

leipo = [Finnish] bread

lemme = let me

Lenino Davinci = Leonardo da Vinci

len'th = length

leprosy doc = lepidopterist

Les Cheneaux = [French] The Snows; chain of islands in northern Lake Huron, east of Mackinac Island and Da Britch.

les raquettes = [French] snowshoes

"Let Them Go, Let Them Grow" = The motto of a widespread sportsmen's initiative to allow smaller bucks to grow larger racks. It doesn't change the meat flavor, just bragging rights.

liberry = library, where all da berry sweet books live

lickmask = litmus

lighten bub = lightbulb

lightnin' pole = lightning bolt

lights = To a butcher, this term means the lungs; a deer shot in the lights is lung-shot.

likecheckits/likechests = lifejackets; required marine safety equipment; "Dose demm woods cops check youse ever' time ta see if'n youse got nuff demm on boot."

likkery spit = lickety-split, quick-fast

lime beans = lima beans

lingo-lookerup = dictionary

linkgauge = language

linsey-woolsey = neither fish nor fowl

lipperty-lapperty = not serious

liquid cork, da = Kaopectate, a product created by the now-defunct Michigan pharmaceutical company, Upjohn, now subsumed by Pfizer, but with global manufacturing still located in Portage, Michigan (Kalamazoo). COVID-19 vaccines are made in Portage, and shipped all over the United States and world.

little tad bit = a very small amount

liveral = liberal

Livertarian = Libertarian

live weight = an animal's weight before dressing out (gutting)

livin' da dream = Ambiguously sarcastic, the meaning can range from "*Tutto bene* [It's all good]" to "My life's a mess and I can't get out."

Lombardi = Vince Lombardi Jr., Football Hall of Fame Green Bay Packers coach

long cooker = oven

long gun = a rifle; sometimes a shotgun

long inda toot' = long in the tooth

loogie, or lungey = *see* "hork"

lookatism = tourism (also pronounced "touronism" or "touroidism"); Limpy calls such travelers "tuursts" lookeeme = a showoff

lookenback or meer = mirror

Lookit! = Look!

look-up books, or d'encyclopeekia = encyclopedia

loon ranger = Person on a lake assigned by the Audubon Society (or the US Forest Service) to monitor and count loons.

loonshit = Slang for noxious, decayed, dark, organic debris that piles up on lake and stream bottoms. In marshes it can be two to four feet deep (and deeper), and difficult to get free of.

love candy = mistress; girlfriend

Lovers Lane = Stuporman's girlfriend

löylyä = [Finnish] sauna steam

LSD = Lake Superior Dick; very real "shrinkage" phenomenon, caused when males step into 30- to 40-degree Lake Superior water. Painful, rarely terminal.

luck of the straw = luck of the draw

lucnee = lynx; these are rare cats in Michigan, but still occasionally seen near Ozark, east of Trout Lake, in Chippewa County

Luffda! = [Swedish] word of exclamation, surprise, or disgust; a close relative of "Oh shit!"

Luffer or leafer = Love her or leave her.

lulu = a crazy person

Lumber Ladies = *see* "Sidnaw"

lumitalo = [Finnish] snow house

Lumpy Dick = An early concoction of pioneer "pudding." Stir dry flour into boiling milk until thick; serve with sweet milk, molasses, or sugar. Related to form of Royal Navy pudding called Spotted Dick. (Don't laugh. It's a bit like pound cake.)

lustry = horny

M

Machilimackinac = (pronounced *Ma-SHILL-uh-mack-in-aw*) Old fort on south shore of the Straits of Mackinac, almost under Da Britch.

Mackinac = (pronounced *MACK-in-aw*) As in Mackinac Bridge, Mackinac County, Straits of Mackinac, and Mackinac Island. [Author's note: Here's a tip: Whether "ac" or "aw," it should always be pronounced *aw*. Not too long ago, Jambe Longue got a text message about the bridge, which autocorrected the spelling to Back-and-Neck Bridge. "Limpy says dat AutoErect jus' a computer tryin' ta straighten youse out." It's nice that he's philosophical about it. Ah, the magic of computers, our marvelous new helpmates.]

mackinaw = A heavy woolen shirt jacket; stylin', eh? (Roughly akin to a pea jacket, jumper, or reefer.)

Mackinaw boat = A wooden boat, eighteen to twenty-four feet long, propelled by oars and/or sails and used exclusively in the upper Great Lakes, c. 1830–1890ish. Could carry surprisingly large, heavy loads of cargo.

Mackinaw City = (pronounced *MACK-in-aw*) Pronounced the same as it's spelled. This time it refers to Mackinaw City, on the south end of the Big Mac bridge. St. Ignace is on the northern side, in the U.P.

made-meat = "SPAM stuff an' fake crap like dat."

made of horror = maid of honor

maffle = to mumble and jumble words

Magic = Earvin "Magic" Johnson, of Lansing Eastern and Michigan State basketball, and the NBA's Professional Hall of Fame. [Author's note: Limpy insists we add Larry Bird here, "'cause 'e was pal a' Magic, an' hard-nose college an' pro."]

Magic Rub = Arnica, a topical treatment that helps alleviate bruising and sore muscles (brand name, Arnicare).

Magnum dopus = What you exclaim when someone makes the dumbest move *ever*.

make-home = homemade

make-ice = To cut ice from a lake, or to flood the ground to make skating ice. This kind of ice takes damn near as much daily care as a weedy garden.

make-meat = Old trapper slang for killing animals for food rather than for their pelts.

makeroot = Make her out; what loggers say when they quit a job, meaning make out my paycheck and I'll be seein' youse.

make-water = urinate

make-wood = to cut, split firewood for fireplace

malbene = no good

mal de raquettes = [French] Inflammation of the shins caused by wearing ill-fitting snowshoes, or not being in shape to use properly fitted ones for extended periods of time.

mammaryacry = mimicry

mandemic = pandemic

maniac expression = manic depression

manimal = mammal

Manistee / Newaygo / Yooper twitch = An erratic jerk-and-retrieve motion with rod and reel, a preferred technique for salmon and steelhead snaggers, and easily identifiable by game wardens using their far-lookers.

manopolkalate = manipulate

mansdysturbate or wymyndysturbate = masturbate

manurecure = manicure

marble orchard = cemetery

marsh hawk, or northern harrier, gray ghost, owl-face hawk, flat-face hawk = (*Circus hudsonius*) This bird is silent, patient, and deadly, somewhere between the size of a crow and a goose. They soar low and gracefully over marshes and fields, and around bodies of water.

Marshy Grass = Mardi Gras

mask = The term for the head or face of a fox, raccoon, wolf, or coyote.

masked media = mass media

maw, or pastyhole = mouth; piehole

mayfly = favorite seasonal food of trout and other fish

mccainic = mechanic; "Somebody can fix stuff."

MD (Mad Dog) 20/20 = Red, grape-flavored cheap wine, 36-proof, favored over champagne in certain regions of the U.P. [Author's note: Have a bottle of this? Youse have youse a real nice flight.]

Meandertalls = "Dose big-head, mean ol' cave jamokes."

meat bag = a trapper's stomach

meat-blindered = vegan

meat cords = zip ties

mebbes trap = tentativeness

medal deflector = metal detector

medicasher = nostrum (quack / fake drug / remedy) salesman; a fake

meer or lookenback = mirror

megrims = the blues, or feeling down; "Youse got da megrims when youse's dobber is down."

Meijers Shifty Acres = Meijer Thrifty Acres is a giant chain store founded by a Dutchman out of Grand Rapids, BTB. The chain most recently opened stores in the Soo, Escanaba, and Marquette, with more allegedly planned in a couple of other locations. [Author's note: A lot of folks in the state call the place Meijers (adding the nonexistent "s"). They used to do the same with Upjohn, calling it Upjohns. Go figure.]

melant = dark, black

melk = milk [Dutch and Low German, which is spoken mainly in Northern Germany, and the northeastern part of the Netherlands] You don't hear this often, but some Yooper Dutch and German families still use the word in this iteration.

'Member? = Remember?

men in da blacks = Amish and Mennonites

mental deflector = metal detector

mentalpause, da = menopause

Merde = [French] "Shit!"

Mer Douce = [French] The Sweet Sea; term favored by seventeenth-century explorers, trappers, and Jesuits paddling or sailing around Lake Huron.

merkin = "Da womyn's tickly t'ing down dere . . ."

Messican = Mexican

Messican corn turd = tamale

Messyitits = Methodists

Meta, den lefta. = Met her, then left her. [Author's note: A very short four-word story.]

metsäsuhde = [Finnish] One's personal relationship with the forest, woods, outdoors.

MG! MG! MG! = A gun-person's rallying call: "My gun! My gun! My gun!" *See* Secondmendmint. [Author's note: Before one of you jamokes gets all hot and bothered about what may seem to be less than reverent talk about firearms, Jambe Longue and I own guns *and* shoot *and* hunt. End of disclaimer.]

Mich'gan's Mississippi = How one Detroit mayor once characterized the U.P.

Mich'gan's Siberia = Another "compliment" for Da Yoop from a former Detroit mayor.

Mich'gan Technonerds = Michigan Technological University students

Michiganderanianite = Limpy's compromise on identity as Michigander, Michiganian, and Michiganite. [Author's note: I don't know why Limpy gets involved in such pointless debates. He'd never say he was anything but a Yooper. I guess he just likes to weigh in and not disappoint, in the same way as if you ask a Yooper for directions, you'll get detailed directions, right or wrong. Yoopers just want to be helpful, even if they aren't exactly sure of the correct answer. Attitude and intent trump accuracy? Hmm.]

Michigan roll = A wad of paper money with twenties or fifties on the outside and all one-dollar bills inside. [Author's note: Consider this an American variation of the Russian Potemkin Village scam, which put importance on appearances rather than substance. When Catherine the Great wanted to see what sort of progress was being made with rebuilding various towns, Minister Potemkin took her for a boat ride to see for herself. What she saw were newly painted and constructed facades with nothing but braces behind them. A scam way back then. The czarina was happy with what she saw. Think willfull blindness.]

microcusses = microgusts

midden = A domestic waste dump, often the focal point of artifact and bottle hunters on sites of abandoned homesteads and around ghost towns and old logging camps. (*Hint*: Look for the first dip in land closest to the old dwelling, and that's most likely where their junk got discarded.)

mightaoughtamebbeshouldacoulda = rather undecided and waffly

mightcanbe = possibly, could be, might be

migrainiacs = "Dose pipples droved crazy by da headakers."

migrainting = migrating; a big headache for all involved

Milbeerkie = slang for Milwaukee

Milkynesia = Milk of Magnesia; "Take dis an' youse can forget youse's problem."

Milliminimals = Millenials

Mining Urinal, da = Nickname for daily newspaper, the Marquette *Mining Journal*

Miniskoick = [Algonquin] with a gun

Minnie Polis = slang for Minneapolis

Minnie Soda = Minnesota

minnieswell = might as well

mishymashy = mishmash; a disordered mess of stuff

mistake law = estate law

misunderestimate = underestimate

mixlectic = "Don't never-ever mix two kinds 'ootch."

mixlexion = state of confusion

mob-up = mobilize; bring in your chums and mates

mode = "Can say dis after youse cutted da yard grasses."

mojakka / galamolyacka = [Finnish] fish soup; and *kalamojakka* is fish stew. Some descriptions say fishhead instead of fish. [Author's note: We'll leave it to the reader to clarify when ordering either in a restaurant or in a private Yooper home. Whatever the translation, fishhead or no, your taste buds won't be disappointed.]

mökkihöperö = [Finnish] cabin silly (our cabin fever)

molly dukes = a male who makes fists like a girl

mollyfy = sex change (from male to female)

Mollyshangle = a Mick-brawl

monkey rock = monkey pox

monkeyry = mockery; "Youse know, like da monkey see, da monkey do stuff?"

Mooch= Steve Mariucci, former San Francisco 49ers coach, and high school teammate and lifelong friend of Tom Izzo when they were at Iron Mountain High School

mooncalf = something twisted, not right

mooner = nooner (but at night)

moonroomed = marooned

moose or paddlehead = Large member of the New World deer family. [Author's note: If you were around in the 1960s and '70s, you may recall the *Bullwinkle* cartoons; this term is still employed for moose by people of a certain age.]

mooseturd = mustard

Mooslum = Muslim; a follower of Islam

mooz = [Ojibwa] moose

moral-eagly = morally, legally

moral rectumlube = moral rectitude

moral turkeytube = moral turpitude

morel = Perhaps the most valued of Michigan's many kinds of edible shrooms (mushrooms). Morel hunters and aficionados are more secretive than gold prospectors (or brook trout fishermen). [Author's note: This is a significant claim for morel hunter secrecy, because the crooked clan of brook trout chasers won't even admit to God where their special spots are.]

morse = A horse mistaken for a moose, and vice versa. Michigan's "sharpshooter" hunters have over the years "mistaken" moose and horses for white-tailed deer.

mortality signal = When collared wolves don't move for a certain amount of time, this signals the animal may be deceased, and biologists then go to find it and investigate.

mortal turpentine = moral turpitude

mossback = trapper who lives way out in the way-back

mosty = mostly

moun' = mountain

mourning heel = moray eel

mousesnap = mousetrap

mousing = night-fishing

mout' = mouth

mout'full = mouthful

mudder = People who drive veeks (vehicles) of all descriptions through mudholes and think this a great hoot!

mudhooks = feet

muds 'n' joes = coffee

mukerta or *makkara* = [Finnish] a kind of bologna ring

mukesick = music

mum = "Youse's mother."

mungle = mangle; mash up

mungo = a garbage picker

mush = To boink; also a term for urging sled dogs onward. [Author's note: I simply report facts; you can connect them any way you wish.]

musher = One who runs with (drives/guides?) sled dogs.

mushroom = "Place where youse's can boink."

muskeg = A kind of soil associated with bogs; consists of dead plants in various stages of decay, with a lot of sphagnum moss on top of a very near-to-the surface water table. Muskeg, depending upon the terrain, can be one hundred feet deep. As you look out on an expanse of muskeg, it looks sorta like a grassy, hummocky stretch of lawny land with occasional islands of trees of varying sizes. Walking on this stuff can be very dangerous. It feels bouncy and sort of spongy under your steps, until you break through. Term derives from *mashkiig*, an Ojibwa word for grassy bog. Look for stunted tamarack, larch, willow, cottonwood, and black spruce as indicators that there might be some troublesome ground ahead. [Author's note: The stark reality and truth is, sometimes one must sneak-foot it across some nasty muskeg stretches to get to the better brook trout waters.]

Muskrat Sally = the local go-to date, available on very short notice

mustausta = there must have been, or used to be

muzzleloader = Single-shot black-powder rifle, like the old-timeys like Dan'l Boone used.

mystery cats = Longtime term for various catamounts, mountain lions, cougars, black panthers, and such, reported all over the state, mostly in the U.P., over the past fifty to seventy-five years. Not much mystery now. Cougars have been confirmed in the U.P., and unconfirmed reports continue BTB, as well. *So far* those BTB have not been confirmed by DNR wildlife personnel. My wife

Jambe Longue saw one just south of Cassopolis (southwest of Kalamazoo and Three Rivers) during the winter of 2020. Author's sightings have been midday near Three Lakes in Baraga County, and not long before midnight, near Ensign in Delta County. Also possible that author and friend and fishing pal, fellow Baldwin Bullshido Bob Peterson, got a millisecondish glance at the tail of one in northern Iron County, many years ago.

N

nail = "Means ta score wit' a womyn, or da man (dependin' who youse is), or might-could also mean da nail use for hook on log in da cabin for ta up-hang da mackinaw on da wall."

naked-face hornet = bald-faced hornets; "Nasty t'ings, hurt like dickens when dey nail youse."

naryhairy = bald

natchhose = nachos

National Rifle Association (NRA) = "Purpose uvda NRA: Get youse ta BMG-BMG-BMG! [Buy More Guns, Buy More Guns, Buy More Guns!] Work pret' good, too, dis way, eh?"

native = Wild trout, not a hatchery-planted "rubber" fish raised on handfed meal pellets.

Native American = "What dat is? Was no pipples here 'fore all dose jamokes crosst over da ice bridge t'ingy in da way-back. We all, ev' demm one-a us, is immigrators 'ere, in 'Merica."

near side / off side = To a trapper, near side is left, off side is right. (Not a political statement.)

'neat' = beneath

neder = neither

neder-eder = Neither-either; sort of a Limpian double-negative take on "neither, nor."

needlepoint = "Da sharp end; you t'ick or what?"

needment = need; "Needment not same as wantment, eh? Youse may want two assholes, but youse onny need da one youse got."

never-wenters = In the days of conscription and military draft, the ones who dodged and never served. "An' now some da beekest flag-wafers is backers of fight all da bad guys in world."

newdatitty= nudity

newtiques = new old stuff; a special for tuursts

nicing on da snake or icing on da lake = icing on the cake

niddle-noodle = bobblehead

niddynoddies, da = "Dose jerky motions dat 'appen to youse's 'ead when youse try nod off an' youse fightin' it."

niffle-naffle = waste of time; something worthless

night = "Dis be daytime for da violators, time dey go ta da work."

night-eye tacks = Reflective tacks to pin on trees in order to mark trails and routes; they light up when hit by an artificial light beam in the dark.

nightnames = aliases; "Names da violators use at night at work. Not dere real names."

Nimrod = From the book of Genesis; a great hunter and king. [Author's note: "The Nimrods" is the nickname of Watersmeet High

School sports teams. Watersmeet is a town of 1,500 in Gogebic County. In 2004 ESPN aired a series of ads featuring the town and its sports, and this led to the school selling $35,000 in school merchandise. Then, circa 2008, the Sundance Channel aired an eight-part series about the town and its boys' basketball team. The "Nimrods" tag was adopted for its teams by Watersmeeters in 1904, a century before the ESPN ads. You can't make this stuff up!]

906 = Yooper area code (pronounced "nine-oh-six"); "Means pipples fum Da Yoop, like da 212s be pipples from New York Sitty (906s an' dose 212s, dey don't mix togedder so good, eh)."

Ning! = to strike someone or something with a thrown object (say, a rock or beer glass)

nipply = nippy, brisk weather or temperature

nips = Wool socks, although up here, the term is generally used to refer to socks of any weight type.

'Nish = Nishnaabe (Anishinaabe); how Chippewas/Ojibwas refer to themselves

nissua = [Finnish] sweet bread, flavored with cardamom [Author's note: A personal favorite!]

nitnoy = [Thai] something small, insignificant, not important; term imported during Vietnam War

nixnay = [Pig Latinish] nix; negative; no

node = already knew

no-go roads = impassable, and often off-limits

noisebox = the radio

nola = [Finnish] zero, none

Nonin = [Finnish] That's it; oh well, all right, then.

Noodle Savage = Noble Savage

noohklar = nuclear

nookick or mealcake = Trapper slang for a sort of cake made from parched ground corn mixed with enough maple syrup or brown sugar that the resulting substance is almost too sweet to eat from the bag—and almost 100 percent carbohydrates. This stuff can serve as high-energy, fast-food trail grub, or boiled with water to make a high-energy tea.

Nordern = Northern . . . Northern Michigan University in Marquette (Marquette County) [Author's note: Not at all sure why, but when some Yoopers say this, it comes out "Nordern" instead of "nort'ern." Go finger (Go figure). Home of da Wildcats. "Nordern" can also mean northern pike (also called hammer-handle).]

normanclature = nomenclature

nort' = north; a direction

Nort', Up = *see* "Up North"

nort'-a'-nowheres = North of nowhere, aka, Bumfuck, Egypt, slang for a largely inaccessible location. Add a distance, say, ten miles north of nowhere, and the location becomes even more specific in its remoteness, and, therefore, unfindable.

northern flicker = dollar butt and/or yellow hammer

northern pike or hammer-handle = (*Esox lucius*) Very good eating.

Nort'scar Polar = Polaris, the North Star; *see* "Bolarus"

nosebag = Logger lingo; lunch bucket made of tin, strapped to the back of a river-driver.

no-sees or starflowers = Certain people who are, for the most part, invisible; or a particular flower, *Lysimachia borealis*, which blooms in May and June.

no-see-ums = Small, hard-to-see, pesky gnats. Some people are *extremely allergic* to dere pesky bites.

No time like pissant = No time like the present.

notlemotle = No-Tell Motel, a place that rents rooms by the hour

nowise = never; no chance

nursie = "Dis 'ow youse address da nurse-womyn, not da nurse-man."

nutfroster = crisp, cold weather

nutshellitous = long story short; a summary, drastically cutting a long story

nuttin' = nothing

nymposygo = nympho; "Dose nymposygo wymyns can kill youse. But youse might-could die 'appy, eh?"

O

oarface = office

oartopsy = autopsy

offen da grid = Off the grid; refers to people living off the beaten track with no electricity and depending only on gas-fueled generators for power. Most off-the-gridders use firewood to heat their places. In a more general sense, the term can apply to anyone who is sort of out there alone, all on their own.

offen-da-road = To operate off paved roads and off two-tracks into the backcountry, sometimes on snowmobile trails or old railroad beds, or even where there are no roads whatsoever.

off-piss = Off-piste, or off the established trail; a skiing term. It's especially important to pay attention to this on groomed cross-country ski trails. Slang-wise, someone who is off-piste is someone who doesn't follow the rules or stay within the lines or generally accepted social norms. Person could be a goofball or an eccentric, or a scofflaw.

Ohiowhiner = a citizen of Ohio

oinkmink = ointment

oldening = aging

olderly = elderly

Old Testiclement = Old Testament

old won-doo, da = The old one-two, which in a fight means a punch followed by a kick—first shot to the nose or mouth, the second, to the opponent's junkal region.

oleo-oops, or margerine of error = a slip, or mistake

onda = on the

on da bend = on the mend

one fella's soup = one fell swoop

one-holer, or two-holer = a run-of-the-mill outhouse, or a fancy, upscale outhouse

one inna boiler = a bullet in the gun chamber, in firing position

one in da hat = gunshot in the head

one-name fame = Individuals who distinguish themselves in some way need only be identified by a single name, which can be their given name, a nickname, or their surname—Madonna, Wilt, Elvis. Usually such fame is reserved for individuals with Yooper roots, but not always.

one-steppers = poisonous shrooms or spiders; "Get bit, or takin' da bite, take one step, an' down youse go, dead as da doornail."

one-trick phony = a one-trick pony; a fake, someone with obvious and serious limitations

onny = (pronounced *OWN-knee*) only

Onty = (pronounced *ON-tee*) Ontonagon, the town or the county

Oompa-Loompas = Those with fake tans from chemicals; "Turns da skin ornch."

oop = up

oopsy doodles = oopsy daisy

oot = out

ootada = out of the

ooten or outen = out of, or away from

ootraw = out raw; nude

openarian = outdoor enthusiast

open carry = To openly carry and display a firearm; legal in some states, not in others.

Opening Day or Da Opener = This can can refer to the opening of any hunting or fishing season, but primarily refers to the opening of firearms deer season, which in Michigan, historically and traditionally, lasts the final two weeks of November (November 15–30).

optional seclusion = optical illusion

orgasmagical = "Changes how youse sees da world, eh?"

Oriniack = [French-Canadian] moose

ornch = orange

ornch scones = traffic construction pylons

orners = orders

'orzee = horse

Osh! = (pronounced *Ohsh*) short version of exclamation, "Oh shit!"

ottery = artery, or "Dat kind a jamoke wants just fish, swim, an' fool 'round in da river."

ouchy = moody or in pain

Ouisconsin = [Old French] spelling for Wisconsin. The name *Wisconsin* derives from "Meskonsing," the English spelling of a French version of a Miami Indian name for a river, now known as the Wisconsin River, which runs 430 miles through the center of the state. Recent scholarship has concluded that the Miami word translates to "this stream meanders through something red," possibly referring to the red sandstone bluffs of the long-famous Wisconsin Dells.

outfitter = One who provides, for a price, equipment, provisions, training, and even guides, for persons engaged in a variety of outdoor activities.

outgo tax = income tax

outstate = Anywhere beyond Greater Detroit. [Author's note: I've never figured out whether this reference point is Detroit looking out, or somewhere else, looking in. But a friend of mine from Detroit once confided, "We never look out from Detroit. There's nothing out there to look at, or for." Reminds me of the New York City as the state of mind I've always characterized sadly, albeit accurately, as "Outside New York is China."]

outstater = anyone not from Michigan

overcast = "Youse t'rew da lure too bloody far."

overwhamming = overwhelming

owly = bad-tempered

ownlifer = a solitary; keeps to self

P

PAC boots / Packs = Refers to felt-lined, insulated boots used in extreme cold and heavy (Arctic-like) snow conditions. The term is a catchall for what the military called ECVB (Extreme Cold Vapor Boots, Type I and Type II). You see these in most extreme-snow, cold-weather places, including the U.P. Most common are so-called white Bunny Boots, which are good to minus-60 degrees Fahrenheit, and black Mickey Mouse Boots, which are good down to about minus-30 degrees F. Type I was developed before the Korean War, and Type II Bunnies were developed for that conflict/war. Both types are now sold in military surplus stores. There are also more recent vintage (nonmilitary surplus) Arctic/Antarctic "pack boots" available to outdoor folk.

Packerbacker = Green Bay Packers fan

Paczki = [Polish] (pronounced *POWNCH-key*) A deep-fried Polish pastry, often filled with fruit and topped with sugar or some kind of icing. A favorite for Fat Tuesday, a sugar high barreling into the dietary wall of forty days of Lent.

Paikoin = [Finnish] here and there

paindammit, da = the pandemic

paint da soles a' youse's boots ornch = Part joke, part safety advice; means to be damn careful when wade-fishing a slippery, nasty bottom–cluttered Yoop river, because if you lose traction, you may quickly drown, and your corpse will be difficult to find. Thus, paint the bottoms of your boots orange to help those trying to recover your body. Funny, eh? Mebbe not.

palitikicians or palitiks = politicians or politics; "Guy get elected, town, county, state, whatever, first t'ing dis jamoke wants do is take care all 'is chums, den dey open hands, open wallets, close dere eyes an' ears, an' get in da quick-hurry ta make da ask, but not deliver on no promises."

pallavertory = meeting place

panfish = small fish that are relatively easy to catch and very good to eat, e.g., bluegills/sunfish, punkinseeds, etc.

pank = Yooper-wide term for flattening and smoothing snow with the back of the shovel, similar to tamping.

pankaka = [Swedish] pancake, served with fresh fruit or jams

pannukakku = [Finnish] pancake, served with peaches and honey drizzled over the top

paper rain = confetti

paradedime = paradigm; "'bout twenty cent," Limpy says.

Paradise = A small town in Chippewa County, and located closest to where the *Edmund Fitzgerald* went down during a terrible November storm on Lake Superior. [Author's note: Across history, November seems to be the month for the majority of the Gray Lady's worst storms.]

parka = A heavy, hooded winter coat, the hood often lined with animal fur or hair.

parking dock = parking ramp

Parking is such sweet sorrow = Parting is such sweet sorrow.

parkoitus = "Parked on side da road, boinkin' in youse's rig or car."

parma = "Dis a cheesy form of da karma."

Parmisan = ptarmigan; "Good eatin' bird live way up north Canuck-land and Alaska, but we don't got 'em 'ere in Da Yoop, or down BTB neder-eder."

pasty = (pronounced *PAH-stee*, not *PAY-stee*) "Not dose swingy-t'ingy little tassels girlies swing on dere basoom nips up dere on da strippin'-bar stage. Dese 'ere are little pies wit' pork, carrots, and rutabeggies, tateys, and, sometimes some udder good stuff. Real Yooper don't eat wit' no gravy goop, nor wit' no ketchup." Pasties are half-moon-shaped to fit on a shovel blade, which was then placed over a heat source to warm deep down in the copper mines. Although it's commonly believed these originated with Finns, that's not true. Probably they were originally Danish, but via India (go finger), and thence from Denmark to England, spe-cifically to Cornwall. "Dese wit' da Cousin Jacks come over ta Da Yoop, brought over da pasties when da mines, dey come over ta make open, eh?"

pasty-an'-da-Pabst = Finnlander's notion of a gourmet meal

pat = Yooper slang for ruffed grouse (*Bonasa umbellus*). Derivation not known, but in Maine ruffed grouse are called pat'ridge, and "pat" may be a further condensation of that. In early America they were sometimes called woodhens. You can hear them "drum-ming" during the year, the sound a part of their mating ritual. The birds come in either a red phase or a gray phase, the difference marked by the predominant colors of their feathers. No matter the phase—or what you call them—the breasts, wrapped in a thick slice of bacon and grilled, are primo eating.

patchouli = "Da hippedy-dippedy wymyns' fav'it foo-foo juice. Might could be some mens wear dis s'it, too, but I don't want t'ink 'bout dat."

Paul Bunyan = "Giant logger, all buncha made-up bunk."

Paulding Light; also Lights of Paulding and da Dog Meadow Light = All these tags refer to a light that appears in a valley outside Paulding, Michigan. Reports of the light have appeared since the 1960s, with popular folklore providing such explanations as ghosts, geologic activity, or swamp gas. [Author's note: In 2010, Michigan Tech students who were conducting a scientific investigation of the light were able to see automobile headlights and taillights when viewing the light through a telescope. The students re-created the effect of the light by driving a car through a specific stretch of US 45. So much for that "mystery."]

pawky = sneaky, treacherous

paydaway = turnpike; toll road

paytriots/paidtriots = "Sort guys don't do nuttin' for country lessen dere money or somepin' in it for dem."

peach = beach

peachgas = beach glass

pear = bear (to a Yooper with a Finnish accent)

pea shooter = any small-caliber firearm (e.g., a .32, .22, or .17)

peen = dull, rounded edges

pelage = fur, hair, or wool covering of a mammal

pelletterie = [French] skins, furs, pelts

pemmican = Indian word for dried, pounded meat combined with dried berries, mixed with melted fat, and made into small cakes. Basic road food of olden times; early trail mix, if you will.

Penguartica = Antarctica

perasspirational = aspirational

permafrost = Ground frozen year-round down to a certain depth. The temporary kind in Yoop is often called ground frost. In cold years, the depth in some locations can reach down nine feet or more, which takes a long time to warm up in spring.

perplex = "One dose huge buildings, got all kinds movie screen onda inside."

personanograppa = persona non grata

perverb = pervert

pestle on da mestle = pedal to the metal

petacure = pedicure

pickers = prickers; thorns

pick-in-da-puke = pig in a poke

pickled cacks (eggs) = bar delicacy in glass jar

piece = Old hunting slang for midday meals carried by shooters.

pignick = picnic

pilke = [Finnish] firewood piece smaller than a *klapi*

pilkunn ussija = [Finnish] comma-fucker [Author's note: While this is not a term common to the Yoop or to Limpy, strikes a nice sour note with my writerly thinking and prejudices. Term refers to one of those "types" of people who can't wait to point out mistakes in written, printed materials. Same folks are rarely so receptive to having their own errors noted for others.]

pimp = salesman

pimp's nest = pince-nez; a style of glasses popular in the late nineteenth and early twentieth centuries. Not supported with earpieces, but rather worn by pinching them at the bridge of the nose.

pineapple guitar = ukelele

pine box payoff, da = One or two months of pay given to survivors of men killed in mining accidents. Most dependents got nothing.

pine olive mole, or P.A.L.M. = pie à la mode

Pine Stump Junction = Location approximately ten miles south of Deer Park (on shore of Lake Superior) and twenty miles north of Newberry in Luce County, where in logging days, mail was delivered for pickup by reps from area logging camps. [Author's note: The old tree marker was still there, last we checked.]

pingswills = pixels; "Dat stuff make you sick watchin' da bloody 'puter."

Pintchered Rocks = Pictured Rocks National Lakeshore, east of Munising

pipples = people

pipplesfloat = life vest or life jacket

piracy = privacy

pirvate = private

pisgoh = the last resort; "Shining crew dey run inta Sonnyboy oot woods, dey give up or run is dere pisgoh."

pismire = an ant; someone insignificant

pisnatchios = pistachios

piss elm = psalm

pissleaks, da = curse of aging

Pistons = Detroit pro basketball team. Basketball is always a grand sport in the U.P., and many Yoopers follow the Pistons.

pitcherbox or idiotbox = TV

pitcher-snapper = camera

pixeldick = computer technical serviceperson

pizza = piece of

pizzamind = "Go give dat jamoke pizza youse's mind."

place-go list = itinerary

plame = blame

planetude = platitude

plank road = A road made of hewn wooden planks two inches thick and eight feet long, nailed to four-inch-square stringers at a ninety-degree angle. Most plank roads were toll roads, the toll typically being one cent per mile for single-animal vehicles, and an additional half-cent per mile for the animal hauling the vehicle. [Author's note: Don't know the rest of the rates, but the concept sounds much like the modern toll structure on the Big Mac Bridge.]

plantatarium = "Dis where vegetarians eat onny weeds an' flowers and like dat-dere weird s'it."

playground, da = king-size bed

plew = beaver pelt

plink = to shoot a small-caliber firearm

plinthera = plethora; a heap; a whole lot

plugly = plug ugly

plumpletude = obesity

plurds = These are plastic bags that blow around and catch in the grasses and on fence lines, the word a combination of "plastic" and "turds." If caught in trees, they are called "witches' britches."

poach = To violate the law and take fish and/or game illegally. A poacher is one who does this for personal gain. The term more often heard in the U.P. is "violator," which means the same thing.

pocket science = rocket science

p'ofessional = professional

poika = [Finnish] son, or boy

pointer trees = The tips of mature hemlocks tend to bend/tilt eastwardly. If you're lost, knowing this can help you find your way to safety. Or not.

poisonhivey = poison ivy; "Youse know, when da skin she get all dose lil' red puffle-ups."

pokelogan = Bay or pocket in a river into which logs may be floated during a drive to move them to a mill.

polar basketball = An outside contest of shirts and skins in January in Da Yoop.

pomplassity = pomposity

Pond, Da = an ocean, or any Great Lake

Ponnyack = Pontiac, town in Oakland County in southeast Michigan; also an auto brand. An Ottawa (Odawa) war chief called Pontiac (*Obwaandi'eyaag*) led an uprising in what became known as Pontiac's War (1763–1766). The violent and bloody armed struggle was against the British in the Great Lakes region because Pontiac and others were "dissatisfied" with British policies. Over time, the war effort spread and became decentralized, and Pontiac claimed greater authority than he actually had, which, according to Wikipedia, led to him being increasingly ostracized. He was assassinated in 1769 by a Peoria warrior. [Author's note: Does this uprising and its antecedents sound a lot like what our American colonies did in 1776, ten years after Pontiac gave it a go?]

p'onoun puzzles = "He/she/it, den dere's he-he / she-she / it-it, and now dere's dey-dey . . . What in da bloody hell is all dat junk aboot? Just tell me youse's name an' use dat, okay?"

pony = a cheat sheet

poofume = bat'room freshener

pooperade = horse parade; "Youse don't never want walk dat street after da horsey's've gone t'rough."

poop sweet = tout de suite; quick

poor man's bank = A pawnshop; in some cases, a dumb man's bank, too, or a trapped-and-up-to-his-throat-in-debt man's bank.

pop = soda; a soft drink

popcorn snow = Small pellets, more ice than snow; but they can sting when they strike exposed skin. "Dose icy lil balls looks like da poppin' corns when dey bouncin' offen da ground, but dey sting like naked-face hornets when dey nail youse's 'ead, eh?"

Popeils = "Dose cheap, junky gizmos used to be sold on da TV by Ron Popeil. Like Pocket Fisherman an' stuff like dat. But dey sure did catchin' da fish, dey did."

popple; also called quakeys = Aspen trees; logged for their soft wood, and used to make paper products, e.g. matchsticks, chopsticks, crates, fences, and many other things. Aspen trees are favored foods of deer, moose, beaver, and snowshoe hares.

pop-up = portable blind used in hunting and/or ice-fishing

portch beer = Brewskis left outside on the porch to keep cool. In winter you have to be careful or it can quickly freeze. The back porch at deer/fish camp doubles as another fridge, or, as Limpy explains: "In winner dat back portch dere ad da deer camp gives youse lots space for brewskis or kecks [kegs]."

porge = da porridge

pork eater = Derogatory term used by French Voyageurs to refer to inexperienced fur traders. "Kinda like callin' dose guys da rookies, eh?"

Porkies, Da = Porcupine Mountains Wilderness State Park in northwest Ontonagon County, west of Silver City, which is west of Ontonagon

porkypine hat = porkpie hat; term used to describe something as impractical, foolish, or having no purpose

portable lightning rod = any graphite fishing rod

posthumans = posthumous

Potomac poisoning = ptomaine poisoning

power oustage = power outage

Po-Yo = Slang for Pope and Young; scoring system for deer taken by bow and arrow.

preachery = "Dis be da preacher's 'ouse."

predaholic = human predators who can't help themselves

predeater = predator

preflab = prefab

preflabulated = prefabricated

preflabutory = fattening food

prefore now = before, in the past

premanure = premature; "'fore it gets oot someplace, sometime youse don't wantin' it to."

preminded = prejudiced

prepast = before

prepellent = Protection you put on your skin and/or clothes before you go outside. Used to keep bugs from biting.

prerumptuassed = presumptuous

pretindians = fakes, pretend Ki-Yis; "Dose jamokes lookin' ta grab some tribe goodies, but ain't tribe members."

pretnur or pert-near = pretty near; close; almost; more or less

prickmedainty = a goody two-shoes

priest = a wooden club used to kill large fish after they are brought to net or shore

prinky = dressy; overdressed, pretentious

prinkly water = prickly water; "Dis kind water looks like somebody pull up da arm hairs. Dese places might can be *real* fishy, so take youse's time an' cover all da prinkly water, 'specially etches an' seams. Dose brookies dey like da etches of dat prinkly water."

prinkolate = percolate

privvyletch = privilege

procrapstinate = procrastinate

prolly or proply or probly = probably

promposition = preposition; "Dose kinda words Finnlanders don't got none any a."

proppity = property

prostate wit' da grief = prostrate with . . .

prostituter = prosecutor

puffer-upper-roller-over = hognose snake

puffle up = swell up

pukefish = Lutefisk (pronounced *LOO-tah-phisk*); Norwegian "delicacy," in this vein, a euphemistic synonym for the disgustingly, sickeningly, stinky crud some humans choose to stuff down their maws (think "delyuckacy").

Pukin = Vladimir Putin, dat whack-job Russian dinkdater guy

pukko/pukka = [Finnish] Sheath knife carried in the old days by men and women, and used for all sorts of tasks. Typically a very hard steel blade with a birchwood handle, often worn on a lanyard around the neck. The old handmade knives are highly valued by collectors.

pulla = [Finnish] Coffee bread. Sweet, but not overly so. Laborious to make (up to four hours). Served nowadays mostly around Thanksgiving and Christmas. Some people add raisins to the dough, and sprinkle almonds on top—of the sugar glaze.

pull-backer, da = anything retractable

pulpie = logger who specializes in cutting pulp wood, popple (aspen)

pump = pump-action shotgun or rifle

Punches Pilot = Pontius Pilate; da bad guy in da Bible, eh?

punkeyes = buckeyes; "Dose loudmout' jamokes fum down Ah-hi-yah [Ohio]."

punktit = pundit

punktitinuation = punctuation

punt = to back off, retreat; run away; disengage

pupples or bupples= bubbles

puppy seeds = poppy seeds

pursht = purse

pushda = To push, or you push; as in "Pushda from ooten da snow-bank dat car."

pushpin = to pinpoint

pussyatrick = psychiatric

Put da cat on da table = This phrase means it's time for a serious discussion and close inspection of something at issue.

put 'er goin' = To get something started, or under way; can also mean to incite or even to inspire. "Once youse put 'er goin', nobody know where she goin', eh?"

Q

Q-Assanone = "Whackjobs and cuckoid chuck-knucks believe weird chit aboot gov'mint. Most'y, dey jus' want youse's money."

quacke = to gag

quackmire = A quagmire; a loonshit swampy area difficult to walk through, but where you will often find ducks and/or geese on small ponds.

quaddle = grumble and complain

quaff = take a drink

quaggle = jiggle

quail = shake in your boots, and/or run away

quantontitty = quantity

quap or quappy = shaky ground

queechy = boggy; bad footing

qweench(ed) = to mash or crush something (or to be mashed or crushed)

queer and peasant danger = clear and present danger

quell = Step on it; stop something "afore she gettin' ootada youse's 'ands, eh."

querimoaner = complainer, whinger

quickcooker, da = microwave

quill pig = A porcupine; "sportsmen" do not kill these animals. However, in an emergency (life-or-death) situation, these provide a fine food, especially their livers, or so some insist.

quim = Da wymyn's "down-dere part."

quink = a domestic goose

quite da soup = messy situation

quonker = kibbutzer

quotician = "Dey allas use udders' words, can't spick for seffs."

R

rabbit = rapid

Radio-Free Trout Creek = Once a well-known enclave of violating activity in the western Yoop, where most of the locals opposed the DNR and made a lot of noise about it.

radish = ravish

raha = Money; the source of this term is unknown. [Author's note: If you see Limpy, ask him. He seems to know a lot about money.]

raise down = To lower, as in "Raise down dose blinds so no pipples seein' us."

rakehell = a no-good, a bum, hell-raiser

Rambo, go = To go batshit, all-in, all-out, no-holds-barred, no-quarter-given-or-expected crazy.

ramdown = steep part of a logging tote road

rammish = lusty

rando = random

Randomland = Anywhere with people. Life *is* random.

range = East–west lines that intersect the principal meridian. Within each township there are a number of six-mile ranges east and west of the meridian.

rapple = raffle

raquettes, les = [French] snowshoes

rat = muskrat

rat du bois = [French] wood rat, means oppossum

read sign = The ability to interpret tracks (sign) left by creatures or humans whom one wants to follow. Yooper conservation officers who go to tracking classes often hear, "You U.P. officers are all damn good trackers." The COs grin. "Yah, if you can't track, how you gonna find people to check?" A very difficult skill to master; borders on being an art.

real Indi'ns = seventeenth- to nineteenth-century Indians, not their modernized descendants.

real tired = retired

rearendedoscope = endoscope

Red = Communist and *Republican* Party colors are the *same*; "How come dat is?"

red devil = red squirrel (considered an extremely destructive pest)

redds = Areas of gravel swept by female trout and salmon on which to plant their eggs for fertilization. For warmer-water species such as bass and bluegills, similar cleared areas are often referred to as "beds."

redeye = rock bass [Author's note: In my limited experience, these are terrible eating, but Jambe Longue's former ninety-year-old neighbor insisted redeyes tasted great just after last ice, or ice-out. Opinions, right?]

Red Owl, da = Name of a chain of grocery stores that once dominated the U.P. "Goin' Red Owl meant one was going grocery-shopping."

Redpop = Faygo-made soda in Detroit, a favorite flavor among many in the old days

Reds = Deer hair takes on a reddish cast in summer, and a gray-black hue in winter. Venison from red-phase deer taken from August through September is said by violators to taste better than venison taken other times of year. 'Course, this is illegal . . . but we're talking flavor, not law.

refutiate = repudiate

reg'lar = regular

rejecticle = to not answer the phone

remembery = memory

repitate = slither like a snake

reptile dicksfunction = erectile dysfunction; "When da ol' snake, he don't work so good."

Republicant = Republican

retardabarian = A backward, vicious individual who is behind the times, and happy to be so.

retired = tired again

reverse court = divorce court

Rez, Da = Slang for Indian / Native American reservations; there are several in the U.P.

rhymantic = "Somebody likes make da nice rhymes."

rice-burner = any motorcycle made in Asia

rice-eaters = The Japanese, Chinese; everybody who hails from anywhere in Asia.

ridgerunner = Yooper who lives in the backcountry, and prefers to spend much of their time "out there."

ridicklisnist = ridiculousness

rieska = [Finnish] rye bread

rifle line or shotgun line, da = Imaginary line approximate to the latitude of Mount Pleasant. Above this line, rifles may be used to kill deer during firearms deer season. South of the line, hunters are confined to slugs and buckshot from shotguns. Shotguns had been the only legal option in the southern counties for decades, but not too long ago, the shotgun zone was changed to the limited firearms zone, and rifles chambered for straight-walled rounds, .35 caliber and larger, with case lengths of 1.16 inches to 1.80 inches, became legal in areas where for decades only shotguns could be used. These weapons are very effective over short ranges, same principle as shotguns.

rig = A general, catchall term for any vehicle or conveyance other than an automobile.

right offen da pat = right off the bat

rime ice = White ice formed by fog freezing on surfaces. Such fog usually freezes to the windward side of tree branches, buildings, veeks, etc.

ripuli = [Finnish] diarrhea; "Youses don't want dis stuff in *any* lingo."

river hog or river pig or cattyman = One who drives (guides) logs down a river.

road-beer or roader = Beer consumed on back roads while driving; once an endemic practice in the U.P., less so now, but still rather common among certain age groups.

roadberg = Chunks of ice fallen from vehicles, the largest chunks being shed by eighteen-wheelers.

road-hunter = An illegal practice by one who cruises two-tracks and back roads with a loaded rifle, looking for "targets of opportunity," usually with a spotlight and with the intent of shooting from inside the vehicle. That's the illegal side of road-hunting. But it is actually legal to look around and hunt this way *if* the weapon is *unloaded* while inside the vehicle, and *not immediately available to the hunter* (meaning *cased and zipped*). If an animal is seen, the driver must *stop the vehicle, get out,* take the *unloaded weapon out of its case, and only then,* the licensed hunter may attempt to make the shot. [Author's note: Oddly enough, Michigan is one of the very few states I'm aware of that allows hunters to shoot directly from the roadbed itself. In most states, the hunter has to move a certain distance off the road before discharging the weapon at prey.] In almost all instances, save exceptions under a few very special permits, it is illegal for hunters to shoot from inside a vehicle.

roadkill = Dead animals on or beside the road, killed by vehicular traffic, and sometimes serving as magnets for scavengers like crows and ravens, eagles, wolves, and coyotes.

road-pop = *see* "road-beer or roader"

road rustlers = Those microscopic organisms hatching from road salt that turn vehicles to rust and thus steal them. Limpy advises: "Get youse a veek fum Assarizona. Dere ain't no road rustlers out dere."

roadside pork = roadside park; "Youse's know what da porkin' is, yah?"

Roads Schoolernerd = Rhodes Scholar; "Dose real book-smart guys don't never want be nuttin' *but* lifelong schoolers, eh? Dey go dis school, den dat school, den 'nudder school . . . Cheesus.

roary = rumor; "Lotta mustard, no meat."

rockify = petrify

rock skimmers = time wasters

rock snot or didymo = A nasty, highly slippery, natural substance that occurs on rocks in some rivers—and *not* just in the U.P.

ronga = [Finnish] huge chunk of wood

rookery = "Da place where ev'body cheat, or colony for birds, like dem great blue herons."

root = route

rosey or cut-throat = Rose-breasted grosbeak (*Pheucticus ludovicianus*); the "cut-throat" name is misleading. The actual color reflects the great flash of bright red—not on the male bird's throat, but on its breast and just under its wings.

rough = roof

round = The term used to describe the height of log cabins, e.g., an eight-round is eight logs.

round forty = Old logging term referring to companies who took their purchased square or rectangular timber stand and, having done what they contracted for, continued to cut and thereby round off the square to enlarge their take, in effect giving themselves an unpaid-for bonus. Illegal practice way back then, and now.

royal bull = six-by-six wapiti bull elk.

rubs = Marks on trees made by bucks (male deer) rubbing the velvet off their antlers and marking their territories for the competition for the ladies. The male whitetail polishes the velvet off his antlers in preparation for battle with other males during the fall rut. As a general rule, the bigger the diameter of the tree so marked by rubs, the greater the chance that it was made by an animal with a sizable rack of antlers.

run = a game trail, a route commonly used by certain animals

runko = [Finnish] Tree trunk, "stern" of a tree; plural is *runkoya*. [Author's note: This word is one for which Yoopers tend to make a rolled "g" out of the "k," so the sound comes out as *rrrRUNgoya*. This may be a local variation in pronunciation, but I've heard it pretty much all over the western U.P. from Menominee County up into the Keweenaw. If you're at a campfire, throwing back some brewskies, and somebody bellows, "Hey dere, t'row to me for da fire dat *rrrRUNgoya*," the request is for a large, unwieldy chunk in the woodpile.]

running dark or running black = To operate a vehicle at night without lights; although this is strictly illegal, it's often practiced by poachers and violators.

runoff or breakup = Spring breakup of winter ice; this process swells rivers, streams, and lakes, and creates all sorts of spring ponds and spring rivulets.

runway = A routinely traveled game trail, often weaving through very deep, very thick vegetation, which serves to keep the animals concealed.

rupper bupple = balloon

rupper fish = Trout raised on pellet food in state fish hatcheries and planted in state rivers and lakes.

rustification = results of oxidation, rusting

rut, da = The annual whitetail mating season, usually in the fall, when males chase females recklessly and relentlessly. Hunters hope the rut will coincide with the firearms deer season—the last two weeks of November.

rutter = Special plow used to create skid roads to skid logs out of the woods to rivers. This is often combined with a regular snowplow. Once plowed, skid roads were doused with water and left to freeze over to make skidding operations easier.

rutting = Mating "for da deers, eh? Pipples don't got no rut. Pipples can do 'er anytime."

Rutyard = Rudyard, in Chippewa County; declares Limpy, who gets around, "One da bestest towns and toughest, friendliest pipples in da hull Yoop. Some real pret' wymyns, too!"

S

Saatana! = [Finnish] *Satan!* Mild expletive, used for bad luck caused by Satan's intervention (slipping on black ice, for instance).

St. Urhu Day = Imaginary saint Urhu alleged to be the Finnish saint who drove the grasshoppers out of Finnish vineyards. His "day" is celebrated on March 16, the day before the Irish have their St. Paddy's Day. Competition? "Youse t'ink?"

Saintvinnyites = The folks who shop and support St. Vincent de Paul stores.

Saint Virus dance = St. Vitus dance

salad bar = A onetime culinary feature of restaurants everywhere; although rarely found today in many parts of the country, they continued in Da Yoop right up till the COVID-19 pandemic raced across the planet.

sammitch or sammish or sammidge = sandwich

sanctionary = sanctuary; sayeth Limpy, "Da safe hideout fum da COs an' udder lawsmen."

sandamanous = sandy

sand handitizer = hand sanitizer

sandman = "Dat silly jamoke, dey say brings da slip [sleep]. Don't know where dis guy get all dat sand."

Santyclause, da = "Once-year deal, eh, for da kittles an' grankittles."

sardinks = minnows of any species; small fish in general

sardoodledoom = drama queen

sasquatch or squatload = a heap; a whole lot

Sassenach = [Gaelic/Erse] An outsider, someone not from the real world. From the Yoopers' view, not from the backwoods. Term was commonly used in the old Hudson's Bay Company that deployed fur trappers and traders all over the Great Lakes region.

satan = a stain (this use strictly a Limpyism)

sauna = [Finnish] Steam bath (correct pronunciation is *SOW-na*, not *SAW-na*). All Finns understand that a hot sauna followed by a dip in the nearby lake or a roll in the snow in the heart of winter will keep you healthy. Brought to the United States by Finns. On Finnish farms all family members bathed together, regardless of gender, and at bathtime, neighbors often dropped by to partake. The "original" Yooper saunas were said to be ten by twelve feet and made of squared logs, chinked with moss and mud, with a shake-shingle roof. There was one door, and only two small windows to let in some light. Inside there was a sheet-iron stove on a bed of flat fieldstones, and other fieldstones were used to cover the stove. Once or twice a week a fire was built in the stove and stoked until the stones turned red-hot. Then water was splashed on the stones to create steam, which rolled up to the roof. The "bathers" sat on wooden benches and rubbed themselves to raise sweat. A bundle of birch switches was used to beat each other's skin red, then the bathers would rush out and roll in snow, or dunk in an icy hole made in the lake or pond, then hustle back inside to towel off, and no doubt partake of some alcoholic beverages.

scaldscold = hothead

scalp = steal, gank, expropriate

scamarous = Onny p'etend like da udder person.

scamdeal = scandal

scamsurance = Insurance for floods, fire, earthquakes, pets, to fly someplace in an airplane, or extended warranties—"any a' dat type a' junk ta get your money."

Scaramouche = [French] buffoon, clown

Scare you in half = Limpy's modification of the saying "scared half to death"

scat = animal feces, distinctive by species, season, and diet

scattergun = shotgun

scavel 'n' gawp = confusing, disorganized speech and talk

schmuck = This verb is regularly used by conservation officers, meaning to strike (and almost always to kill) a large mammal with a vehicle, or for a vehicle to strike or hit anything, including other vehicles. [Author's note: This use rang odd in my ear in this context from the first time I heard it twenty-two years ago, and it still does today. In English the word *schmuck* means a foolish or thoroughly contemptible person. In Yiddish, presumably from which the word migrated into English, the actual word is *schmok*, which means "penis." I'm not even going to try to unjumble the thinking in this word plasticity. I report it for what it is, and leave it at that, and you to your own speculations.]

schnitz = cut, dried apples

schoolteacher = teacher

scoodle = to skip a flat stone across open water

scrape = An area of ground pawed clear down to mineral earth by bucks, who urinate on the cleared spot to mark territory. These markings are often in an extended line over several hundred yards, and meant to serve as a warning to other male deer.

screechers or skreekers = all gulls and seabirds

scromp, scrompulate = *see* "rut"

Scurrier and Hives = Currier & Ives, makes dose $$ birt'day cards

scutiter = somebody who does mindless tasks

Seccatareyah State = Secretary of State

Secondmendmint = The US Constitution's Second Amendment— the constitutional right to own weapons. Also called Two Eh, 2Eh, 2A, and MGMGMG. In part because of all the hunters up here, gun rights are a *very* big deal across the U.P. [Author's note: There are times when I am speaking to some of the most ardent gun rights advocates that they seem to fervently and quite genuinely

confuse the Second Amendment with some sort of Second Com-
mandment, which seems to read: "Thou shalt never give up to no
one, at no time, in no place, under no circumstance, youse's gun,
so help youse Gott."]

Seen horns? = "Youse seen any bucks [male white-tailed deer]?"

seen-saw = saw; past tense of "see," but often used incorrectly, as
in "I seen da game warden." (I suspect most Yoopers would be
astonished by how often the game warden seen them.)

seiche = A form of tidal wave that sometimes develops under special
atmospheric and weather conditions on the Great Lakes.

Seizure salad = Caesar salad

Seney stretch, da = An eighteen-mile stretch on M-28 from the
stoplight in Seney west to Shingleton. The road defines the word
"straight," and often is boring. [Author's note: This stretch of
highway is not without the possibility of amusements, and mammal encounters with wolves, black bears, deer, and/or moose. I
once went into the DNR office in Shingleton and asked if they
had a map of moose sightings. The fellow, who identified himself
as a biologist, advised, "Just keep driving back and forth on M-28
till you hit one." That's your serious advice? I asked, and he just
nodded and said, "Yup."]

serpelingo = fast-talking grifter

set = Trapper's trap, baited and positioned to take an animal.

set-line / trot line = A static, baited line used by fishermen who are
not present; an illegal practice.

"Seventy-eight, you're great; seventy-nine, you're mine" = In days
when the interstate speed limit was 70 mph (it remains so on some
stretches), there was considerable debate among drivers about how

much "latitude" a Michigan State Police officer would allow drivers. A friend of mine was at a school hosting several officers on a career and safety day, and when he asked them over lunch what their rule of thumb was for 70 mph on the interstate, they piped up in a chorus, "Seventy-eight, you're great; seventy-nine, you're mine." Word to the wise: Stick to the speed limit and there will be no need for a debate. If you attempt to engage in a "debate" after you are pulled over, you will without doubt find it the shortest and most polite, yet entirely one-sided, conversation you'll ever have.

sex dent = sextant

sex sock = condom

sext books = textbooks

shadesis = oasis

shadow clock = sundial

sheds = Antlers that are dropped annually by deer and moose, usually in winter. There are avid collectors of such sheds, and some are quite valuable.

She's makin' snow = Nature's giving us a snowstorm.

Shinook = Chinook

Shockereel = Moray

shooting lane = Sighting area for a hunter. Some nimrods "enhance" their lanes by illegally cutting down live trees on public/state property. [Author's note: They can cut down all the trees they want on their own land.]

shooting light = Enough ambient (natural) light to safely see and fire at game. The actual hours are calculated for each day, each year, for deer season, printed in the annual hunter's guide, and aggressively enforced.

ShortS = *see* "Strohs"

Shotanabeer! = Yooper version of "Cheers!"

shounta = shouldn't have

shovel = footrest for government and construction workers

show = A movie; if asked, "Want go show?" it means, "Would you like to go to the movie theater?"

show-butts = retreat, run away

shrink-head = psychiatrist

shrinkle = shrink

shrooms = mushrooms

shuggle = shake

shush fund = hush fund

sicken, or cackles = chicken, to some

side-by-each or side-by-next = Yooperese for next to each other, or beside each other.

Sidnaw = (pronounced *SID-na*) Town in south Ontonagon County; site of Henry Ford's first U.P. project. Ford built a lumber camp with bunkhouses, steam heat, and laundry services. Locals called Ford's loggers his "Lumber Ladies." During World War II, Sidnaw hosted a work camp for German POWs. The POWs were housed and worked at the site of an old logging camp.

sign-lookage = sign language; "Got ta see signs if want unnerstan' an' talk dat lingo."

silk and money = milk and honey

Silver Spider = An ounce or two of lead soldered to a large hook, an illegal tool used to illegally snag fish.

simpulate = simplify; "You'se know, sometimes gots ta dumb 'er down, eh?"

sin-honest = honest as sin; an honest person

sinman = cinnamon

sinnercourse = intercourse

sin-ta-order = senator

sirple = syrup

sissy = pine siskin

sisu = [Finnish] (pronounced *SISS*-oo) The all-fight, no-quit determination to see something through with iron-jawed will; mettle, guts.

s'it or chit = This is "shit" in Yooper patois. There is a road in the Calumet area called Cowsit Flats. It was once a grazing pasture for cows, and, of course, translates to Cowshit Flats.

S'itcongo or Shitcongo = Shitcago, Chicago (pronounced *Chacaga*)

s'itfaced = shitfaced; drunk

s'ithole = any place Limpy finds disagreeable, or anyone who disagrees with him

s'ipment = Cologuard package; "Test comes in da mail, an' youse send in da specimens by mail, a somewhat s'itty transaction."

s'itoric = shitoric; foul rhetoric

s'it-tick = shit-tick; that very last millisecond before shit happens s'ittin' ice-bullets = shitting ice-bullets is to be afraid; fearing something

s'itymphony = The nearly continuous scream of sirens and all kinds of discordant sounds, all the time in s'itties.

skankerous = nasty

skeptic tank = septic tank

skidder = device to haul logs

skid road = Old logging road used to move logs in winter when most logging was done.

skimmer = sleigh, sled

skintilla = chinchilla; "Tiny little critters dey usta make da wymyns' fur coats fum."

skip = elevator cage in underground mine

skip ice or skiff ice = The first light, thin layer of ice to form in the fall or during re-freezes. The term may have developed from the thin "skin" of ice that first forms.

skippitty rope = jump rope

skookum = [Chinook jargon, an extinct pidgin] Powerful; this Chinook jargon is still in use in the Pacific Northwest, but was also used in logging camps in the Upper Midwest. Still hear it today, though rarely.

skrakkled cacks (cackleberries) = scrambled eggs

skrakklomelet = omelet

skreeking = "Some nasty sound like dose weird pipples run dere finger claws down chalkboard."

skullkology = psychology

skullpert = culvert

skunkmentous = strong animal smell

skunkolo = somebody who's gone bad

skunkweed = Cheap, low-grade marijuana that when lit is wonderfully redolent of faintly fresh skunk.

skunky = Something gone bad; usually in reference to beer flavor.

skybangings = fireworks

skybunk or skybald = good-for-nothing, useless

sky sweat = rain

slambambimbo = "Onna dose fast wymyns. Youse know, dey say no, dey mean mebbe. Dey say mebbe, dey mean yes. Dey say yes right off, dey got sure da slambambimbo." Also, a professional woman in a certain old (and, in at least one US state) legal profession.

slap-slaps = windshield slappers (wipers)

slender years = young

slickery = slippery

Slidikin! = "By God's eyeballs," a very old exclamation, heard these days only at the occasional Renaissance Fair.

slip = sleep

slip-one, lay-two rack, da = bunk bed

slippys juice = KY = "Wah, da slippys juice for da youse-know . . ."

slow-dump = unload, disinvest quietly, phase out

slow-roller = A vehicle creeping down back roads at speeds slower than walking. Typical behavior of folks looking to spot game; "Mebbe take shot fum da rig." Although slow-rollers could be something as innocent as leaf peepers, slow-rolling is sure to attract the curiosity of your local game warden or conservation officer, *especially* after dark falls.

slug box = glove box, where keep extra slugs for da t'row-down gun

slumburg = suburb

slumgullion = Common logging camp and trapper meal, comprised of watery meat and veggie stew. Sometimes cooks would create crust of hard tack on top; *see* "hard tack."

smarmky = greasy, oily; a combination of "smarmy" and "sneaky"

smell test = "If it smell like s'it, den . . ."

smelt = Species of small fish that live in various large lakes and swim up and spawn in creeks in spring. Excellent table fare, deep-fried in fresh oil. There used to be a huge social event around smelt-dipping at night by torches and flashlights, with whole families taking part, but runs have seriously diminished since the last great runs in the 1950s, '60s, and '70s.

smeltering = sweltering

smile-good = feel-good

smoked sights = Gunsights blackened by candle soot to eliminate shine or glare.

snag = Dead tree or brush pile in a river, or to attempt to illegally catch fish by impaling them with large, unbaited hooks.

snagging = Deliberately hooking a fish in the fin or side or anywhere on their bodies other than in the mouth. This is illegal, and those who get caught are heavily fined. All sorts of illegal lures and devices are used in this effort, the best known (and fully illegal) being the Silver Spider, an ounce or two of lead soldered to a large hook.

snarlyyow = An aggressive dog, often a Staffordshire terrier; *see* "spitbull."

sneakers or tenners (in the western U.P.) = tennis shoes ("trainers" to da Brits)

sneakulator = land speculator, landgrabber

sneercasm or snarkasm or scarcasm = sarcasm, depending on how deeply it cuts . . .

snickersnee = knife fight

snicksters = scissors

snifflries = the common cold

snog = snow fog

snottygoster = dishonest person

snowboarding = Now an Olympic and world professional sport, it's said to have originated in Da Yoop.

snowbug = snowmobile

snowchucker = snow shovel

snow cow = moose

snowflakes = Snow buntings (*Plectrophenax nivalis*); circumpolar birds that sometimes drop down into northern Michigan to escape Canadian winters, usually in large flocks. They are six to seven and a quarter inches, with a pale-brown crown and back with long black and white wings and white underside. Drive slowly; they often lift up from roadsides and ditches in large flocks and do not evade very well.

Snow-Go-Bye-Fast = festival held at Lake Gogebic

snowhead or dump duck = A bald eagle; the latter name derives from our national birds hanging out at waste dumps, refuse piles, and landfills. [Author's note: Ben Franklin argued vociferously for the wild turkey to be selected as our national bird over the bald eagle. Makes me wonder how large and stinky dumps were in Revolutionary times!]

snowpack = Cumulative buildup of snow over the seven- to eight-month course of northern Michigan winters.

snow roller = A device attached to plows in order to flatten and pack down snow.

snow scoop / Yooper scooper = Push device used by Yoopers to push and clear away snow.

snowshoe = Either a kind of hare, or the things you put on your feet to travel in deep snow.

snowsnake = A long stick thrown down ice runs by kids; also said to be an invisible creature that can knock you off your feet in winter. Began as, and continues to be, a Native American pastime (for tribes where they have snow).

snowsticks = cross-country skis

snowstuds = Tires that have metal studs implanted to provide traction in winter conditions.

snowtire = Specially made for winter driving in snow and ice. Interestingly, narrower tire areas often better off-road in deep snow than are wider ones.

snow t'rower = gas- or electric-powered machine, used to move snow

snurd = A snow turd; chunks of dirty gray or black snow that fall off the frames of vehicles.

Soapy = G. Mennen Williams, hugely popular Democratic governor who served six two-year terms from 1948 to 1960. Graduate of Princeton, the University of Michigan law school, and heir to the Mennen fortune.

social meanies = social media

sockdolager = Something large and imposing. [Author's note: This word has an interesting history. According to the Worldwide Words Website, researcher Barry Popik found this more detailed speculation in the issue of the *Chicago Daily Tribune* of March 19, 1893: A writer in the March *Atlantic* gives this as the origin of the slang word "socdolager," current some time ago. "Socdolager" was the uneducated man's transposition of "doxologer," which was the familiar New England rendering of "doxology." This was the Puritan term for the verse ascription used at the conclusion of every hymn, like the "Gloria," at the end of a chanted psalm. On doctrinal grounds it was proper for the whole congregation to join in the singing, so that it became a triumphant winding up of the whole act of worship. Thus is happened that "socdollager" became the term for anything which left nothing else to follow; a decisive, overwhelming finish, to which no reply was possible. The particular claim to fame of *sockdolager* is that a close relative of it was supposedly almost the last word President Lincoln heard. In Tom Taylor's play *Our American Cousin*, there occurs the line "Well, I guess I know enough to turn you inside out, you sockdologising old man-trap," and as the audience laughed, John Wilkes Booth fired the fatal shot.]

Somebody step on duck/spider? = Who farted?

somepin' = something

somewither = somewhere

Soo, Da = Sault Ste. Marie, Chippewa County, eastern U.P., Michigan. Soo, Michigan, is separated from Soo, Ontario (Canada), by the St. Mary's River. The two cities are sometimes called Da Two-Soos. [Author's note: Western Yoopers like to "tease" that the eastern U.P. isn't really part of the U.P. Eastern Yoopers just roll their eyes.]

Soo Canoe = Cadillac automobile; "Like youse see when da *Ki-Yis* get shit-faced, buy new one after dere gasino check get cut at end of year."

sound shooting = Shooting at sounds and suspected animals, rather than shooting at what one actually sees and has identified as legal game. Often a sign of an inexperienced hunter, and a practice that has led to killing and wounding of other hunters.

Soupy = Milton Supman, known professionally as Soupy Sales, was an American comedian, actor, radio/television personality, and jazz aficionado. He was best known for his local and network children's television series, *Lunch with Soupy Sales* (later titled *The Soupy Sales Show*, 1953–1966), a series of comedy sketches frequently ending with Sales receiving a pie in the face, which became his trademark. From 1968 to 1975, he was a regular panelist on the syndicated revival of *What's My Line?*, and he appeared on several other TV game shows. During the 1980s, he hosted his own show on WNBC in New York. Hugely popular all over the United States, but dearly beloved in Michigan.

sout' = south

space track = orbit

spaceys = heroin addicts

Spacific or Pissific Ocean = Pacific Ocean

spack = six-pack (of beer)

spaloon = A combination beauty parlor–saloon. [Author's note: Yooper businesses are about what sells, not set categories. We get our fresh chicken and duck eggs from the auto parts dealer (as well as swampers). And we really like a certain restaurant that also sells ammo (not firearms). The tables sit among old wooden display cases with glass tops, all of them at one time filled with ammunition for rifles, shotguns, and various pistols. Furthermore, I should point out that guns are pretty much seen as tools by Yoopers, and as tools they expect owners to use safely, and with common sense.]

Spamish = Spanish

sparency = transparency

spare root = square root

sparkle-arkle = anything shiny and eye-catching

sparklers = Yooper high-fashion term for bright, clean white socks paired with dark pants.

sparrow hawk = American kestrel (*Falco sparverius*)

spatchcock = chicken split in half and roasted

spearing = Legally taking various game with spears. For some fish and game, spearing is either entirely illegal, or illegal at certain times of year.

specs = Speckled trout, brook trout (*Salvelinus fontinalis*); actually a char, not a trout at all.

Speedy Crick = nickname for Rapid River

spendough = cash

sperm of da moment = spur of the moment

spew or yak = vomit

sphagnum = A form of moss most associated with extreme acidic soils and conditions, especially muskeg bogs. Sphagnum is a major component of peat, and can be used as roofing insulation on cabins, or as toilet paper, or as fire starter. In fall the moss turns bright yellow or red.

spic' = speak

spic' wit' da heavy tongue = This usually refers to someone with a Swedish accent. [Author's note: How Swedish is "heavier" than Finnish eludes my ear.]

spikehorn = A young male whitetail with single-point antler on each side.

spitbull = pit bull, aka Staffordshire terrier

spitula = spatula; Limpy adds, "Don't know why, but way back dere was real good-lookin' Englander girlie singer name a Spitula Clark. Why you t'ink her folks give 'er dat handle? Once knew Iggy guy dey called Da Goose, in da way back, an' 'e was *allas* talkin' 'bout dat Spitula girlie."

SPK = The three main Yooper spices/seasonings: salt, pepper, and ketchup.

splacknugget = oddly formed junk rock

splaination = explanation

splatisdics = statistics; "Dose pipples just guess, t'row numbers on da wall, act like dey got answers."

sploppets = mud splashes all over a vehicle

sploomph = a splash, perhaps as much as a jigger

splotchety = brindle

splother = a mess

spoffish = fussbudget; picky

spokenabalary = vocabulary

spongebone = ligaments, tendons

spontaneous rambunction = spontaneous combustion

spoon dropper = "Da kind nap where youse put da spoon on da back
a youse's hand an' close da eyes, an' when da spoon fallen off an'
makes da noise, da nap, she's over."

spoon meat = "Meat youse cut up real teensy-small for Granpa an'
udder pipples wit' da bad teet."

spoor = animal sign

spose = suppose

sposeta = supposed to

spruce = lie

sprucer = liar

sprucie = Spruce grouse (*Falcipennis canadensis*), beautiful, stupid
birds; can walk right up to them. Illegal to hunt and they taste bad.
Per our friend Limpy, "Dey taste like s'it, but in a pinch dey'll
eat." (Illegally, natch.)

spud = Tool used by ice fishermen to bore holes. Most are hand-
operated, but there are some motorized augers as well. Also a term
for potato, same as it is in many places.

squaintance = acquaintance

squamush = to enthusiastically squash or flatten something

squank = sudden muscle cramp or pain

squawhirly = undecided, halfway—like a squirrel crossing a road

squaw wind = Unexpected warm wind in the middle of a long, frigid period; think Chinook in the dead of winter.

squeakety cheeses = Squeaky cheeses, e.g., *Juustoleipa* or *Juustoa* [Finnish]. Also, facetious term for Finnlander yogurt.

Squeat! = Let's go eat! *See also* "gweet" and "Jeet?"

squeezened = squeezed

squeezercordian = accordian

squid-pro-crow = quid pro quo; "Youse know, dis for dat?"

squishy = dubious, doubtful

squonktail = someone covered with ugly dark warts

squrls = squirrels; includes fox, gray, and black squirrels, but not red devils (red squirrels)

staggerly = To move haltingly, unsteadily; doesn't always mean the person is inebriated. Can be caused by extreme age, or by icy, poor footing.

stand = *see* "blind"

standing ovulation, or da clap-stand = standing ovation

standstill crane = sandhill crane (*Antigone canadensis*); "Dese are dose big buggers, sound like da petradickkills (pterodactyls), got da nasty tempers too. Pipples eats 'em out ta Da Dinkotas."

[Author's note: I find it fascinating that the Latin name for this bird utilizes the name Antigone, daughter of Oedipus—yep, *that* Oedipus, from Greek literature and mythology, including three plays by Sophocles in which Antigone appears. I swear: How *do* these things happen?]

starflower = (*Trientalis borealis*) Common plant in the northwoods. A species no botonist has yet messed with genetically to make it smaller, larger, etc. One of those plants people see but don't see, and thus, largely ignore. *See* "no-sees."

statehood = In Michigan history there have been several attempts by Yooper pols and pals to make Da Yoop its own state. Once such fictional place was to be called Superior. In the summer of 2022, similar gibberish was making the rounds in the bars—that after the November election, Yooper pols would make yet another push for statehood. We'll see. They should send a delegation to Washington, DC, and Puerto Rico to get some tips . . .

statue of imitations = statute of limitations

steak = state

stealth wealth = "Stuff gov'mint don't know youse got."

steamer = Pile of bear or wolf crap so fresh there's still some steam rising off it.

steelie = A steelhead; once thought to be a type of rainbow trout, now considered to be separate species. Great fun to catch on a fly rod.

Steven Steelbird = Steven Spielberg

stewage = sewage; "Youse know, when da camp skeptic tank gotten da leak an' youse smell da raw stewage?"

stickfire = wooden match

sticktight= form of bur that sticks to clothing and dog fur

stiff garden = cemetery

stiff time = rigor mortis

still-and-clear = Offhand weather report: "She still snowin' an' clear oop ta my ass, eh."

still-hunt = Find a track in the snow, follow it slowly, stop a lot, look around a lot. Also called stalking.

stinkabator = burn barrel; incubator

stinker = bloated, rotting corpse

stink eye = the evil eye; a kind of curse

Stique or Steek = Manistique, in Schoolcraft County

stirrup = Bread made from fat, flour, and water in a Dutch oven, or on a stick, suspended over a fire.

stocking's tray = stock in trade

stomp = stop

stomp sign = stop sign; "Youse got make cackalation if youse can make it t'rough or have come-stomp 'cause your relatives might be comin' 'on udder way. Dis da same deal wit' da red lights."

stone gun = stun gun

stonehard = absolute, final

stoneskipper = shallow person

stoont = student

stoopid or Yoopid = "Stupid" with emphasis; "Yoopid" is Yooper-stoopid! Extremely, irretrieveably stupid!

stop-and-go = Traffic light; some counties in the U.P. have none—zero, zilch, nada.

storeplus = surplus

Stormy Kromer = Famous wool hats, choppers, and other winter clothing; great, warm, durable products. Many Kromer hats get passed down from one generation to the next, and still do the job. Originally made in Milwaukee, but now Yooper-made in Bessemer (Gogebic County) in the western U.P. [Author's note: I've been wearing Kromers since 1958—sixty-four years. No, *not* the same one.]

strapped = armed with a handgun

strike-bait = A type of bear bait set near roads to help track animal movement.

strike dog = Lead bear dog, the one with the best nose. They ride in the truck bed and when they pick up a scent, the hunters stop and let them loose to follow the bear's scent, and when they hear their strike dog singing in strong pursuit, they release more dogs to join in the hunt. Legally only seven dogs can run a bear at one time.

string bog = Land form typical in Seney area, a treeless area over a peat bottom. [Author's note: I've been told—but am so far unable to verify—that in some of these places, there were fires so hot a hundred years ago that the heat killed everything, and much of it has yet to recover. Perhaps in another hundred years there might be seedlings. I won't be around to see them, and chances are, neither will you.]

string cheese = A tubular-shaped Swedish-Finnish cheese, largely tasteless, but filling; also called rubber cheese by detractors.

stringy = skinny, thin

stripeyed = (pronounced *stripe-eed*) striped

stripeyed 'orse = striped horse (a zebra)

Strohs = longtime popular beer from Detroit, called ShortS in code (*Strohs* spelled backward)

stubbgly = What farm fields look like after cutting—stubbly and ugly.

stumpjumpers = "Extreme Wood Ticks stay oot dere beyond da pail in da deep woods."

stupidcide = suicide

stupidfy = overstimulate

stupidstistion = superstition

Stuporman = Superman; "Listen, dere ain't no such t'ing lessen you put some jamoke on da drugs an' he t'ink he can do stuff he can't do."

Sturgeon River Wilderness and Sturgeon Wilderness Gorge = Wild country in western U.P., north of Sidnaw. The river cuts a gorge up to three hundred feet deep, the deepest in the state. Sadly, hikers fall to their death around the gorge from time to time.

styleghettos = stilettos

Subito = [Italian] Hurry up, step it up, step on it, faster.

subitoer = fast afoot

sucfleur = [French] flower-sucker; a hummingbird

sucker = "Anybody follows da rules."

suckispants = sycophant

sugarbeeter = flatlander; an outsider

sugar jerky = fudge

Suicide Hill = Ski-jumping hill between Negaunee and Ishpeming in Marquette County.

sukas = [Finnish] (pronounced *SOO-kas*) Limpy adamantly claims these are dregs in coffee or tea cups; apparently this can also refer to dregs in a glass after wine or other alcoholic liquids. [Author's note: I don't see this in any Finnish or Swedish dictionaries, but this book is about Limpy's language, so I leave it in and you can judge for yourself.]

Summer, Indi'n = Da warm-up after first freeze; sometimes in October, but not always.

summertime = "Two, t'ree days July mebbe."

sun bath = "Get sweated up, let da sun dry youse offen."

sunlift = sunrise

sunrise side = the eastern U.P.

sunshows = sunrises and sunsets

sunsink = sunset

sunsink side = the western U.P.

suomi = [Finnish] homeland

Superior = Name proposed by the stillborn movement wanting to designate the U.P. as the fifty-first state. [Author's note: In French, *supérieur* means upper. Thus, the English translation of "superior" does not mean "better," referring only to altitude/elevation/latitude, Superior's waters ultimately flowing downward into the others.]

supper = Evening meal (not "dinner"); "In Yoop dere's breakfast, lunch, an' den dere's da supper."

surp = syrup

surplus, army = "Dat cheap, used gov'mint stuff."

swale = Linear area or depression (means low area), often swampy or wet, found between dunes and/or beach-ridges. In the U.P., the term is loosely applied to almost any small swampy area.

Swamp Angel = Originally this meant a girl from Republic (west of Marquette), but now it's generally used to describe any female hailing from the Yoop's more isolated areas.

swampball = Extreme version of feetsball (soccer) played in mucky swamplands in winter and/or spring by da Finns back in Da Homeland.

swamp buck = An almost mythical creature in deer-hunting circles and lore; means a buck that lives in severe isolation deep in the swamps, grows to immense proportions, and is so far in the way-back country, it's almost never seen by hunters. Very elusive, and their meat is said to be tough and hard to chew.

swampergrass = asparagus

swampers = Knee-high insulated rubber boots worn in most seasons; called Wellingtons in Great Britain. Original swampers were worn mainly in spring and fall mud seasons, but now there is Thinsulate, meaning they can be worn even at 30 below 0.

Swampus = Mythical invisible beast, description unavailable. May be a form of *wampus*, which means opossum.

swan = big white bird, tastes for shit

sweater = "Kinda work make youse sweat da bullets."

Swedeling = anyone of Swedish descent

Swedish = official second language of Finland

Swedish butter = da oleo

Swedish Finns and Russian Finns = Finnish immigrants were sometimes divided into two distinct groupings, the Swedish flavor said
to be sober, friendly, and churchgoing. The Russian types were
also called Drunken Finns, said to be savage in their drinking habits, lovemaking, and just about every other aspect of their lives.
The distinction between these two "clans" or "sects" is not much
discussed anymore.

Swedlingish = Swedish; "Dat goofy language."

swedo = pseudo, fake stuff

Sweedo = Speedo

sweet blood, da = diabetes

sweet grass = Indi'n prayer weed; spread da smoke, don't inhale it.

Swenglish = combo of Swedish and English

swhirledwind = whirlwind

swither = to hesitate

swithery-slithery = sexy wymyns

swoofts = really smart people; "Da ones t'ink real fast."

syrt = quicksand

T

tachy = fast, quick

tag = take

Taggers or Tags, da = Major League Baseball's Detroit Tigers

Tahq or Tock = Tahquamenon Falls (Upper or Lower) and the Tahquamenon River

takin' wood = Yooper term for cheating at cribbage

talons = long claws (fingernails)

tammy = Tamarack tree (*Larix laricina*); a small- to medium-size deciduous conifer (sheds needles every year). Tammies turn bright yellow in fall before dropping their needles. Wildlife use them for food and nesting. The trees need full sun and do not like shade.

t'ank = thank

taple = table

taptop = laptop computer

targoyle = gargoyle; "Youse know, dat sticky stuff youse stick da hand in, can't pull outen?"

tarpaper = work hard

taser = lightning ride; "When da jerk cop zap youse, h'it like ride on da lightnin' pole."

taut = thought that's focused and not all over the place

tautose = To be set in one's ways; stubborn, inflexible, unwilling to consider changing.

tavern = A bar or social club; also often serves as a small village's main gathering place and information exchange center.

taxedbook or sextbook = textbook

TB = TV; television

T-bone = To strike another vehicle amidships at a ninety-degree angle.

T.C. = Traverse City, home to a large population of political liberals up in northwest Lower Michigan. To some, it's Michigan's version of the land of fruits and nuts.

tea = hot brown water

teabird = black-throated green warbler; "Dere call, she sund like dis: *Youse-want-me-make-youse-tea?*"

Tech = Slang for Michigan Technological University in Houghton, home of the Huskies.

tek or teg = take

telebooty = "Dis what mos' dose TV preachers allas after."

tell-tales = gossips

tell-upons = squealers, narks

tell-youse, da = the boss, the person in charge, the one who gives the orders

temporary undisorientation = "Da good woodsman never lost, jus' sometimes mebbe little tad-bit undisorientated."

tenner = ten-point buck

'tention or tenshin = attention

ten year, from now back = ten years ago

terms = "Whatever da jutch say."

terrain, sharp = stark terrain

Terra incognita = [Latin] "Da place where youse is lost, don't know where da 'ell youse is. Dis usually happen in da deep dark cedar swamp on cloudy day."

terrorist = anyone from another state or BTB (downstate)

Tervetuloa = [Finnish] Welcome! This is commonly found on wall and door signs, especially in the western U.P.

Teutonic = titanic

t'ever = whatever

Texgass = Texas

tharma = catgut

There it is here = There it is, or here it is.

thrums = "Da fringes on da buckskin duds; youse can win $$ at open bar trivia wit' dis one, eh."

t'ick, t'icken = thick, thicken

ticket = thicket

tickets = playing cards

tickletale = embellisher, bullshitter, storyteller

tight pattern = to shoot five rounds with an iron-sighted rifle into a two-inch group at one hundred yards

timberdoodle = American woodcock (*Scolopax minor*), a migratory bird; also called bog sucker, hokumpoke, and Labrador twister. Wrap breast in a slice of bacon and grill for a delicious meal.

t'imbleberry = Thimbleberry; a wild, sweet-sour fruit that ripens in August in rocky areas. Gatherers can be even more secretive than morel pickers and brook trouters; both groups are legendary for never surrendering the locations of their favorite and most productive spots.

tin boat = anything crudely made or poorly manufactured

t'ing = thing

t'ink, t'inking = think, thinking; a mental process

t'inkbone, da = brain

tinkle da furry bone = tickle the funny bone

tinnedfoil = tinfoil

tippy = Turkey vulture; just watch them fly, and pay attention to flight feathers at wing's end.

tip-up = Ice-fishing rod device with a spring trigger which makes flag pop up when a fish takes the bait.

tip-up towns = Big lakes where there are aggregations of ice-fishing shanties, sometimes in the hundreds. The original tip-up town was on Houghton Lake, BTB, in the middle of the state.

Tirana = Toronto, as prounounced by Canucks, and many Yoopers, too.

t'irsty or try t'roat = thirsty or dry throat

toast butts = taste buds

tock-shock = toxic

toda = to the

toe claws = toenails; *see also* "finger claws"

toetag = da final hashtag

togedder = together

Toivo No-Pack = "Too poor buy even da beers."

Tommy = Tom Izzo, of Iron Mountain, longtime men's Michigan State Spartans basketball coach tongue bashing = tongue lashing

tool = dual; or duel

tool around = cruise in your car or on your motorcycle

toolies = the backwoods, da bush, boonies, etc.

toom = empty

topcooker = burner on stove

topunnertail = upside down

tornado chow = trailer park

torpeeksi = [Finnish] enough

torpor = wild pig "wit' da big husks"

tote road = A "road" made for moving timber to rivers and logging camps. Same as a skid road. Sometimes constructed with logs laid side to side like a floor, and if done this way, called a corduroy or cord road.

totta kai = [Finnish] of course, naturally; sometimes the term used is *tutysti* [Finnish]

touchography = topography

tough bark = Trapper slang for someone with a very tough hide; one who refuses to be stopped or killed.

tour da fords = tour de force

tourons or touroids = tourists

tow = pull; "When youse in da ditch in da snow, youse need a pull, but youse call tow truck."

town name = Da womyn's question; "Holy wah! How come in fish-camp youse call me 'sweetheart,' an' in town youse call me 'hello'?" Dis like at last call in bar an' all da ones becomes tens, eh?

toy sojers = various right-wing militias

Toy-VOLL-ah = Toivola (Houghton County)

Tradio = Radio classifieds program where people call to buy and sell stuff. Very popular and long-running program in various parts of the U.P.

trail, da = Can refer to footpath, game trail, or snowmobile, ATV, dirt bike, bike, or 4WD path of some sort. Everyone is always on some sort of trail through the woods. Experienced outdoor people know that large mammals also like to walk on those same trails, where the going is easier.

trail of taut = train of thought

transchannelchanger = transgender

trapper sammitch or sammidge = Trapper sandwich, made of honey, oats from oatmeal, peanut butter, and jam or jelly, all mixed together and smeared between bread slices. Very high-carb, high-calorie; full of energy to keep you going, especially in the cold. [Author's note: I make mine with uncooked oatmeal, and often carry these food supplies in my fishing pack, *but* as a type II diabetic, one sammitch will knock my blood-sugar levels into the right-field seats for the next week!]

trashers = Parties in the woods where everybody brings a bottle and everything gets dumped in one large can or plastic barrel and mixed together; sometimes called "grassers" BTB. [Author's note: Fortunately, unlike ancient Rome, out in the woods one is surrounded by a massive vomitorium; there's no need to seek out a special building.]

trashies = New clothing items purchased with holes already in them, worn mainly by those in their late teens, and twenty-somethings.

trashpesting = Trespassing is at times a sort of local sport or game in the U.P. With so many armed people, especially during hunting seasons, this can be a high-risk, potentially lethal activity.

Traver, Robert = *see* Voelker, John D.

treachery = treasury

treaty areas / treaty rights = Geographic areas where rights to fish and hunt and gather were specified and guaranteed for Native American signees in the 1836 and 1842 treaties. The state and the tribes continue to negotiate and adjust as the years go by.

t'ree = three

treehugger = derogatory term for an environmentalist

treeing the bear = Hound hunters strive for their dogs to drive their quarry up a tree before killing it, partly so they can evaluate if there are cubs, or if the animal is of legal size and age. Coon hunters and their dogs do the same thing with their quarry.

treepounderize = tenderize

t'ree-stepper = "Dis be my ol' daughter-law, late son Jerry's ex-wife, Honeypat. She kill you same as poison shrooms, spiders, or snakes, but do it slow-like, 'cause she want bleed youse of all youse's stuff 'fore youse's dead."

t'ree tee = 3-D

Treetown = Nickname for Cedarville in Mackinac County, in the eastern U.P.

Tren-AIR-y = Trenary in Alger County

Trenary Toast = "For dippin' inda joe or tea, udderwise, she breakin' youse's teet' an' youse be spittin' oot youse's Chiclets."

t'rew = threw

Tribal = Card-carrying member of a "federally recognized" tribe. All tribes have qualifications and requirements for membership. Just having Indian blood isn't enough.

tricker = trigger

trickered-out = Tricked-out, meaning fancied-up to the extreme; hot, heavy, and fancy beyond adjectives. Can apply to anything from cakes to snowmobiles.

trickoration = trickery, cheating, sleight-of-hand

trigger guard = da guy wit' da gun

trillibub = a trifle; something unimportant

trimental fuckwit = To Limpy, anyone who is emotionally, intellectually, *and* physically defective.

trine = trying

trinkin' = drinking

Triple Eh, da = The famous and notorious Triple A Road which runs west and east across northern Marquette County. Starts not far south of Big Bay, and good luck finding your way across, night or day.

t'roat = throat

t'roat pump = throat bump; Adam's apple

troll = Some people claim this to be a common Yooper term for anyone from BTB, but I have rarely heard it used anywhere other than in the eastern U.P., around St. Ignace.

Troop = Michigan State Police officer

trotline = Set-line with multiple hooks and baits, usually secured to the bank or to jury-rigged float.

t'row, t'rown = throw; thrown

t'row-down = An old shotgun or rifle carried by serious violators. This weapon can be discarded in the event "da dang game warden starts pull over youse's truck." Also means to point a gun at another human; "ta t'row down on some jamoke."

T'row spoon in corner = dead [Author's note: This comes out of Finnish culture, when people had their own spoons for eating, and when someone passed, so much for dat spoon.]

tru = through

trufax = True facts; a confusing, misused term that often means not facts for which there is widely accepted evidence, but "facts" which may in fact be only personal feelings, and stemming from only a single, biased viewpoint.

trut'-mout' = truth-mouth; a truth-teller

try-t'roat = dry throat; thirsty

tulitikku = [Finnish] wood tick

t'underbowl; also terlet = toilet

t'undermutters = thunder mutters; sounds of a distant storm

t'undertires = aggregate term for aggressive off-road tires that make a racket back on paved (hardtop) roads

turd = third; a number; "Youse know, firs', skund, turd, eh?"

turdy-turdy = A .30-30 caliber gun; the famous old Model 94 Winchester lever-action carbine deer-hunting rifle. At one time the Model 94 was *the* deer gun in Michigan.

turfquake = earthquake

turnhead = a good-looking woman

Tutto bene = [Italian] Everything's good, it's all good . . .

tuuli = [Finnish] wind [Author's note: Be careful not to confuse the *tuuli* with the toolies (backwoods, boonies); a big *tuuli* when one is out in the toolies can bring a very nasty experience.]

tuursts = tourists

tuzzymuzzer = tough guy, a scrapper and fighter

twatoos = "erotic" body inkings

Twatter / twat = Twitter / tweet

tweener = running between home and camp, or camp and outhouse

twill = or twon't, eh?

twinkies = gutless cowards, guileless goofballs

twinkwads = oddballs; "Pipples can't be counted on, eh."

twirly = figure skater

two-blanket night = Old logger's term; the more heavy blankets one needed, the colder the night.

Two-Hearted River = Great and scenic trout water in Luce County; "Dere ain't no such t'ing as da *Beak* Two-Hearted, da river dat Hemingfake-guy wrote 'boot; dat guy was beak fake about U.P., only spend one week in 'is hull life up 'ere."

two-stepper = Any venomous reptile; there are very few in the U.P. Here and there you'll find some small massasauga rattlesnakes, which, while venomous, do not qualify as two-steppers for most bite victims.

twotoyant = [Pidginized, Yooperized French] for *tutoiement*, the act of using the affectionate, intimate *tu* (you) with someone. *En fran-çais*, *tutoyer quelqu'un* means to use *tu* when speaking to someone, rather than *vous*. Use *tu* only when speaking to a person you know well, or who is one's own age.

two-track = Any rutted dirt road in the woods, and/or through fields and swamps, often with a hump of grass/weeds in the center. Does not refer to just any dirt or gravel road; it's a specialized term. Sounds like "two-drack."

tyflume = typhoon

typogramphical = topographical

U

udder = other

U-ee = Sudden 180-degree turn; a complete change in direction.

uglicity = unattractiveness

uh-oh! = Duck!!

unanimalate = inanimate

unbe = die

unclelament = inclement

Undeniable Discharge = Dishonorable discharge from military service. [Author's note: This official stain can stay with an individual for a lifetime.]

undenturd = undeterred

underground-looker or metal deflector = metal detector

undocumental landagrabs = undocumented immigrants

unfang = punish

unfeminate = not girly enough

ungood = bad

ungustable = tastes terrible

unhoused = homeless

Union, Da = automatically refers to the Teamsters; *see* "Jimmy"

unit = snowmobile [Author's note: No clue where this neutered term developed, mayhaps other than in a manufacturer's accounting or sales department. Still, it's a term you hear from time to time.]

United States Forest Circus = US Forest Service

unmew = to free

unner = under

'unnert = hundred

'unnert-yard rule = Limpy explains, "Most s'ittyots drive up 'ere, an' so scared da woods, dey can't stand ta hunt more den 'unnert yard fum dere trucks."

unorder = disorder

unparallelized = not parallel

unsaniac = maniac

unsplain = make an excuse

unthaw = thaw

unvite = uninvite

unwhereabouts = unknown, lost, missing

U.P. or Upper Peculiar = terms for the Upper Peninsula (as are Da Yoop and ATB)

up da line = Yooper term for advancing in the high school sports championship tournaments. [Author's note: Every team wants to go up da line, though in my day, that led ultimately three hundred miles south to the championship game in East Lansing, or wherever a sport's final was being hosted. Goin' up da line remains a very big deal, and for many kids up here, it's the highlight of their young lives.]

up da road = An indeterminate distance to a destination or location.

up-down box = elevator

up-hang = How some Yoopers may phrase hanging up an item, e.g., "Gone up-hang youse's goat [coat] or leaverdere on floor, get stepped on?"

Uplanders = "Dose pipples fum da Upper Lower Peninsula. Dey still trolls, like rest dem BTB jamokes."

Up North = *Up North* is a term of romantic and realistic relativity. It means different things to different people, depending on where you live now, and often, where you were born and how you grew up. What is it about the North that captivates so many folks? Here's an excerpt from my novel *The Snowfly* (Lyons 2000): "North, I knew down deep, was where I belonged, north being as much a philosophy as a direction or destination. You knew when you were there, or you didn't. Those who couldn't feel it and embrace it, generally tried it only once. You fit, or you didn't. The basic law of nature was the law of the unexpected. In the woods, or on a fast river, you were attuned to this; at home, in your job, in a relationship, you were not, yet nature pertained in all settings to all species in one way or another. North was the home of the unexpected. North spawned chilled chaos, yet warmed my heart."

Upper Lower = The top part of Michigan's Lower Peninsula

Upper Peninsula State Champions = You'll see this sign outside some towns; I'm not sure if it means 1) The U.P. is considered its own state; 2) in some sports the teams don't qualify to go up da line (which means downstate), so this is the end of the road for the team's competition; or 3) everybody in Da Yoop knows that being the best in the Yoop ought to be equivalent to being best in state.

Upper Peninsula State Fair = Held in August, always in Escanaba. [Author's note: Not sure how this event qualifies as a "state fair," except state $$ are involved. And this may be changing, or already has. There seem to be differing opinions on the financial link, but newspaper ads for the 2022 event still called it the U.P. State Fair. So dere.]

up to 'is dankles, or up to 'is dangles = The first phrase means "up to his ankles," and the second refers to being up to other parts of one's male anatomy.

urban ducky = urban decay; "Dose shitties, dey alla time fallin' 'part, eh?" [Author's note: Apparently, our dear Mr. Allerdyce doesn't look around closer to home, because there's plenty of places coming unglued up here, too.]

urn = urine

Urine Mountain Club, da = The Huron Mountain Club, an exclusive private club more than a hundred years old, located north of Big Bay in the far northern reaches of Marquette County.

Urine Mountains, da = The Huron Mountains, north of Marquette, stretching west into Baraga County.

usta = used to

uvda = of the

uvem or uvdem = of them

V

vaginatarian = a very limited and restricted diet

valetine parking = valet parking

vanny = Vanilla extract; Limpy advises: "Bottle of da back-pocket for backpack emergency snort."

varmint = Any critter, human or otherwise, that causes any problems, real or imagined.

veek = automobile or truck; a vehicle

velvet = Soft fuzzy covering on moose and deer antlers as they first re-grow after winter. They get rid of the covering by knocking their antlers against trees and posts. [Author's note: The sloughed-off material *stinks!*]

venterrifical = ventricle

Vernors = The archetypal Detroit soft drink, Michigan's own pecu-
liar-tasting (many say "unique") ginger ale.

vicey versey = vice versa

vihta = [Finnish] Birch switches (with leaves) used in da sauna. Why
switches, you may ask? Because birch leaves are thought to contain an oil that can help relieve pain. The oil is also said to have
anti-inflammatory properties. Whipping the skin with birch twigs
increases circulation, which can help to relieve pain. [Author's
note: It's a Nordic thing, okay?]

violets = A term woods cop Detective Grady Service uses to label
Fish and Game law violators.

virgin = pristine, mystical and rare; or an extinct critter, much discussed and rarely seen

vitch = a bitch; "Dis kind uv camp light, make by fillin' tin cup wit'
da bear fat [or any animal fat], insert twisty rag or wick, light wit'
da match, an' poofs! Youse gotten seff da camp light."

vocablahberry = vocabulary

Voelker, John D. (pen name, Robert Traver) = Michigan Supreme
Court justice, fly-fisher for trout, novelist, and tale-teller. This en-
try is super long because (as CBS correspondent Charles Kuralt put
it) Voelker was "a great man," and a deep lover of trout and trout-
fishing. He once said, "Trout fishing is the most fun one can have
outside a bed." Indeed. If you don't know of him, check out this
bio. *Anatomy of a Murder* was the book that gave John Voelker national prominence as a writer. It was the fifth book he had written,
but the fourth to be published (after *Troubleshooter*, 1943, *Danny
and the Boys*, 1951, and *Small Town D.A.*, 1954). It was the first
of his books to make the best-seller lists across the country. John
Voelker was born in Ishpeming on June 29, 1903. He claimed to

have written his first story, titled "Alone All Night with a Bear in a Swamp," at age ten, and he always added that after this title, all he needed to do was add the "woof!"

The future author began developing his skill as a writer during his years at Ishpeming High School, and further honed them at the Northern State Normal School (now Northern Michigan University) under the instruction of A. Bess Clark and James Cloyd Bowman. Following graduation from the University of Michigan Law School in 1928, Voelker began practicing law, first in Marquette with the firm of Eldridge and Eldridge, then in Chicago for three years with Mayer, Meyer, Austrain and Platt. He established his own practice in Ishpeming in 1933. Following graduation from law school, Voelker served briefly as an assistant prosecuting attorney while with Eldridge and Eldridge, and was elected prosecuting attorney of Marquette County in 1934. He served from 1935 through 1942 and again from 1945 through 1950. He served as Ishpeming city attorney in 1943 and 1944.

Throughout his years as prosecuting attorney, Voelker also maintained a private practice. After his defeat by Edmund Thomas of Ishpeming in the 1950 election, he returned to full-time private practice. In 1952 Voelker was asked to defend US Army lieutenant Coleman Peterson, who was accused of the murder of Mike Chenoweth, owner of the Lumberjack Tavern in Big Bay. After a six-day trial, the jury returned a verdict of not guilty by reason of temporary insanity. Voelker turned over the events of the trial in his mind, and in 1953 he began tinkering with the idea of writing a novel based on the trial. He was not able to take the idea very far because he was working on the final draft of *Small Town D.A.*, which was published by Dutton in 1954.

Following the publication of *Small Town D.A.* he devoted all of his writing time to *Anatomy of a Murder*. By early 1956 he had completed a revised draft of the novel and began sending it to publishers. The publishers were not impressed, and the rejection slips began to pile up. Sherman Baker, his editor at E. P. Dutton, had moved to St. Martin's Press, so he sent the manuscript to Baker. Baker liked what he read, but also realized that the pretrial portion of the novel was too long and needed to be substantially pruned. In September 1956 he flew to Marquette and spent the weekend with Voelker, cutting and refashioning the manuscript so that the trial was the centerpiece of the novel. Voelker then prepared another draft, the third, of the novel for formal submission to St. Martin's Press.

On December 31, 1956, St. Martin's notified Voelker that they had accepted *Anatomy of a Murder* for publication. Coincidentally, Governor G. Mennen Williams telephoned *that same day* to offer John a seat on the Michigan Supreme Court to fill the remainder of a vacant term. Mr. Voelker was sworn in as an associate justice several days later. At that time Michigan law required justices to stand for election at the next statewide election following their appointment to an unexpired term, so in addition to his court work and making revisions and corrections to the novel, he had to campaign for his court seat. He was elected by a resounding majority.

Publication of *Anatomy of a Murder* was scheduled for mid-September 1957. However, the Book-of-the-Month Club chose the novel for one of its alternate selections and requested that publication be postponed until January 1958. St. Martin's acquiesced, and the book was published in early January 1958. It was an instant success and quickly climbed the best-seller lists, staying there for over a year. St. Martin's planned to have the book turned into a Broadway play and then a motion picture, and asked John Van Druten to write the play. Van Druten completed a rough draft of the script before he died in December 1957. Eventually Elihu Winer wrote his version of the play, which had its premiere at the Mill Run Theater in the Chicago suburbs in 1963.

Meanwhile, St. Martin's had made the film rights available, and they were finally acquired by Otto Preminger. All of the filming was done in Marquette County, and the film was very successful. [Author's note: People still talk about the Hollywood crew and all that went on way back then, like it was yesterday.]

Finally assured of an "adequate" income (which he doesn't quantify or define), Voelker resigned from the Michigan Supreme Court in January 1960 to devote his time to fishing and writing. He was quoted as saying, "Others can write my opinions, but no one else can write my books." Some people would dispute his contention; many of his opinions have been termed the most literate ever to be handed down from the Michigan high court.

Trout Madness, his fourth book, was published in 1960, and was followed by *Hornstein's Boy* (1961), *Anatomy of a Fisherman*, with photos by Robert Kelley (1964), *Laughing Whitefish* (1965), *The Jealous Mistress* (1967), *Trout Magic* (1974), and *People Versus Kirk* (1981). He also wrote several articles, mostly essays on fishing, and, for a brief time, a column in the *Detroit News Sunday Magazine*. Voelker once said in an interview, "As a kid, my mother taught me to go to the library and read, read, read. I think reading is one of the best ways to educate kids." Not that his own reading started out with the classics: Voelker reported that he plowed through the Robber Boys and Horatio Alger stories first. It was his opinion that reading makes us familiar with real words and real language, not technically narrow judicial words and phrases, which he said made so many judicial opinions "so god-damn unreadable."

In 1991, Voelker had a heart attack while driving, and died. His vehicle came gently to rest against a snowbank. God's cushion, no doubt.

[Author's note: I bumped into the man twice in my life—once up in the Big Bay area while I was pat hunting, and another time one evening on the East Branch of the Escanaba River. I knew who he was, but being an aspiring writer myself, and a hunter/fisherman, I was pretty sure he wanted to be left alone to do what it was he'd set out to do, and so I left him alone both times, keeping out of his sight so as not to interrupt him. I sometimes regret not bothering him to introduce myself, though I'm not sure why this is. One thing I know: He and I were both attracted to books, and reading, as well as to the same sort of woods and wilds in the U.P., and all of this, I imagined, amounted to a bond between us, albeit unspoken. As some great philosopher (or unknown barfly) once said, "We regret only those things we do not do, *und sie weiter*" (in German, "and so forth").]

Voi kauhea! = [Finnish] (pronounced *VOY-gow-ee-ah*) How awful or terrible!

voluntold = A volunteer who is "ordered to volunteer." [Author's note: The old Soviet national airline (now Russian national airline) Aeroflot used to specialize in these for passengers. Aeroflot crews did *not* eat them.]

Volvovilles = towns where Yuppies hive and thrive

vomelet = omelet made with any little green bits in it

vowel movement = bowel movement

vulturator = "Dose jamokes allas after da roadkill."

W

wafers = wavers, as in flag-wavers

Wah-huh! = Exclamation of surprise; similar to Wow!

wall-hanger = Any legally killed fish or mammal big enough for a taxidermist to mount and hang on your wall in a prominent place where it can be appropriately admired, worshipped, and bragged about.

wall-talkers = "Da drunk guy at da bar talkin' ta da wall in urinal troughs."

wampus or jibby = To some, these terms refer to opossum. Right now, the only possums in the U.P. are known to be in southern Menominee County. [Author's note: Given the recorded reality of global warming (and never mind debating its cause), it seems not unlikely that the opossums' range will spread further north into the U.P. as the climate continues to moderate.]

wank-wank = a jerk

wankywonks = Limpy's explanation: "Dose know-it-all guys, da talkin' heads, dose pretty boys an' girlies fum da TV. Da ones wit' da fancy degrees."

Wannago? = Want to go?

wannigan = A logging camp mess hall; and cookshack, often built on a raft in a river or lake.

washboard = laundry

waterhole = well

water skunk or fats = lake trout

way-back, da = Da boonies; what Australians call dere Outtendaback.

way-close-down-dere-looker = microscope

way-far-oot-'n'-way-da-heck-up-dere-looker = telescope

wenchful t'inkin' = wishful thinking

wet'er = weather

wet'er-guesser = weather forecaster

wet-ink pen = fountain pen

wet squid = unsatisfying

whackerjobs = whackjobs, fools, crazies

Where at? = Where?

Where da hollyhocks are? = Meaning, where's the bathroom, outhouse, etc. [Author's note: In the old days, before indoor plumbing, civilized country folk planted hollyhocks around the outhouse/privy so that guests might ask politely for the bathroom without saying a dreaded word. Times appear to have changed.]

whichever = which

whinge = whine, complain, bellyache

whips = Term which seems peculiar to far western U.P., referring to stands of young aspen (popples) and/or birch saplings, the kind that when you try to push through, they keep slapping at you annoyingly, like little whips.

whistle trout = carp

white dirt = snow

whiteout = Conditions of heavy and blowing snow, making it impossible for drivers to see ahead, a condition sometimes called CSS (Can't See Shit). If you've never driven in a full whiteout, you've never really driven in severe and scary winter weather.

white rain = snow

whizzer = wizard

whoopee cough = whooping cough

whoopee crane = whooping crane

whoorgantick = organic

whores laugh = horse laugh

Whuh? = What?

whunever = whatever, or whenever, interchangeable

Widdershins = "Head inta da sun."

Widdershins und deasel = [German] This means to walk toward the westward-setting sun, or eastward into the rising sun.

widower-eats or gassyerole = Soon after a wife dies, casseroles and other food start to arrive at the widower's home, in the hands of women—some married, some divorced, some widows. [Author's note: This cultural practice is not limited to the U.P., or even to the state of Michigan.]

wife-beater = sleeveless T-shirt

wifey, or hugby, da = the wife, or the husband

wilderness = A relative term used to describe a place or area in which human beings are outsiders, and animal and plant life reign supreme. Another way to look at this is to say that in a wilderness, human beings are potentially on the menu.

wildlife viewing area = Explains Limpy, "Da best see da bears an' stuff is at da local dump, at night, but don't look for da dump ducks [bald eagles] in da dark. Night's when da bears come oot." [Author's note: Regarding bears: You *never* hear them coming toward you, but you almost always hear them leave, especially if they have been startled.]

willowstripper = First real cold spell of the fall, which strips leaves off the willow trees.

windbowlers = bullshitters

wind chill / heat index = Add moving air to the ambient temperature and it will either increase or lower the temp. A 10 mph wind at 32 degrees Fahrenheit makes it feel much colder than the temp (wind chill). And 10 mph at 93 degrees F makes it feel hotter (heat index).

windfall = "Why pipples use dis word? Da wind don't never fall, but it knocks stuff down, an' dat's what windfall is, stuff knock on keester by da wind. If tree blow down in river, pipples 'ere, we call dis da sweeper."

Windigo (Wendigo) / Windigo Psychosis = A sort of cannibal, originating in Native American legend. Someone who is frozen inside and kills and eats his family; must be killed to stop him. [Author's note: This is a real and very serious psychosis. Several cases are reported in medical literature.]

windpanker = bullshitter

wind pudding = What you get to eat when you have no food.

wingnut = scofflaw, weirdo, troublemaker; not quite right in the head

Wings, Da = Not cooked, nuclearly spiced, and hotted-up Buffalo chicken wings, but *Da* DEE-troit Red Wings, who perform on skates, not on plates.

winner = winter

winner in Da Yoop = Limpy once said, "Winner up 'ere jus' like summer, 'cept not so many leafs on trees an' mebbe tad-bit more white dirt."

winterkill = The biological cost of winter, often expressed in the number of dead deer in a winter season. The worse the winter, the more deer that die. [Author's note: The literature on this topic suggests that an average Yoop winter kills one hundred thousand white-tailed deer; a severe year kills in excess of two hundred thousand. When wolf opponents complain that the wolves are eating all of the U.P.'s deer, they forget the toll of winter—or the many thousands of deer killed by vehicles year-round.]

Wishingsleazy = Washington, DC, "da nation's crapital."

Wissywig = WYSIWYG: "What youse see is what youse get."

witcha = with youse

witches' britches = plastic bags caught in trees; *see also* "plurds"

witchful t'inkin' = wishful thinking

wi'th = width

wit'oot = without

wobbledeytop = bubblehead

woggle da mind = boggle the mind

wolfie / woofie = Eastern gray wolf; also called the timberwolf. After extirpation in the 1960s, wolves worked their way back to the U.P. from Minnesota. [Author's note: The wolves were first officially observed in 1989 as reestablishing themselves, although some locals insist there's always been a small native population of wolves here. Other locals claim "da DNR trucked dem in, in da dead a' night, an never told nobody nuttin'," e.g., without informing the public. Sheesh. Pipples dey belee anyt'ing dey hear, or see on dat Fakesbook t'ing.]

womyn, wymyns = woman, women

womynsizer = womanizer

Wonderbreaders = the well-heeled and well-off

won-doo-dree, da = the only dance rhythm allowed in the Yoop

woodpanker = woodpecker

woods cop = *see* "conservation officer"

woods rat = squirrel

Wood Tick = Term for those Yoopers who prefer to live remotely, as in off the grid.

woof = *see* wolfie / woofie

woolly = anything vague, or confusing

woolover, da = pullover sweater

Wopera = EYEtalians' opera

Woptalian or Wop = Italian

Wop top = *see* "fredora"

Wop worms = spaghetti; pasta in general

worm-noodles = vermicelli

wort' = worth

Wreckanomics = Reaganomics; "Stuff named for da president Ronnie Wreckan."

wreckrenational = recreational

wrinkle metal = aluminum foil

wuchas = What are youse . . . ? (Wuchas doin' wit' deer rifle in front seat of truck in July? Sonnyboy see you, he gone wring your neck.")

wunta = would not have, or won't

Y

yackofftiffs = Adjectives; extra words thrown in to increase word count, or to help the writer grope for a description he can't quite reach. [Author's note: Some great writers have adapted Shakespeare's dictum regarding lawyers—"First, kill all the adjectives!" I say kill most of them, and keep a few around just to remember what they are.]

yah = yes

Yah, eh! = Yes! (emphatically)

yah-sure or you betcha = Sure, all right, okay; a tepid response, at best.

yahwis = youse bet

yammeryapper = someone who talks too bloody much

yap pal = false friend; all words, no action

Yappy Hour = Happy Hour; "When da whiskeys flow an' da tongues get loosed."

Yard, Da = Rudyard, Chippewa County; home of the Rudyard High School bulldogs.

yardbirds = free-range chickens

yards, da, or deeryards = Areas where deer congregate in winter; they usually feature heavy white cedar stands where there is thermal protection and meager food sources afforded to the animals by virtue of the heavy overhead cover. Some deer migrate long distances to these yards every year (e.g., from just south of Munising farther south to Stonington Peninsula, east of Rapid River).

yard sign = Palitikal advertising crap; "Once Yoop yards were filled wit' da Ross Perot signs. Den dey got cluttered up wit' Ron Paul signs, and da most recent been Da Donald MAGA signs. Who will be next up in da yard-sign game?"

Y'at? = Where are you (at)?

yellow light = "Dis means it da demm gas pedal or youse's gone get stuck at da red light."

yellow snow = Warning: Do *not* eat dis junk.

yespert = "Expert get paid agree wit' da yahoos 'oo 'ires 'im."

yestreen = last night

yokyopeli = [Finnish] nighthawk, or someone who is a night owl and up all night (like many career violators)

YFL = Yooperese as a First Language

yink-and-yank = yin and yang; "Dose China funny guys, like we had da Martin an' Lewis, Laurel an' Hardy, an' guys like dat."

yogi or yook = To spin 360 degrees on ice, either on foot, or in any kind of vehicle. The term *yook* didn't come into use until sometime after 1960.

Yoinks! = exclamation of surprise

Yooper = As explained earlier regarding Da Yoop, this seems to be a fairly recent term for describing anyone *born* in the Upper Peninsula. Being a resident doesn't make you a real Yooper. [Author's note: You can't be the real deal *unless* and *only* if you are born and raised here; if you move away at one week old and live away for the next thousand years, you're not a Yooper. And, if you were born in Calumet, and moved to Galiporny at age ten, you still are not a Yooper—Half-Yooper, maybe. This rule is final, which is singularly unusual, because most rules, regulations, and laws are thought by many Yoopers to be loosely suggested options, like diaphanous guidelines.]

Yooper Banana Belt = *see* "Yooper Riviera"

Yooper Dome = Log-built, domed, multiuse, indoor arena at Northern Michigan University in Marquette. Concerts, political rallies, football, basketball, etc. [Author's note: Perhaps the largest log cabin in the world? Certainly it's the most preeminent.]

Yoopered = A pejorative term used by non-Yoopers to describe a drunk. [Author's note: Technically, this severe condition appears to be located somewhere north of "dead drunk."]

Yooper golf = crap-shooting

Yooper hammer = screwdriver

Yooper lightning = arson

Yooperlites = Curious stones that illuminate under a black light. Found all around Da Yoop, but mostly along several Lake Superior beaches. They are quite the fad currently. [Author's note: Leaverites to me.]

Yooper newspapers = Mostly these days they have shrunk to a quarter-page of national and state news; a quarter-page of bitch letters to the editor; and six pages of sports, including bocci ball league and bar-sponsored horseshoe and dart league results. [Author's note: A little editorial speech here—If all politics are local, it seems to follow that the same can be said for all news. But when you have local newspapers with minimal staffs and no official editorial positions, what you have mainly are cash-cow advertisers, not legitimate newspapers, and a community anywhere in this state, or this country, without its own local newspaper, like a community without its own library, is only the shadow of a real community.]

Yooper Opener = White-tailed deer taste best when their fur color changes from winter gray to summer red, and Yooper violators traditionally (habitually?) start their illegal harvests around the Fourth of July.

Yooperphonics = The oddities and intricacies of the Yooper "patois."

Yooper Riviera = Southern U.P. along Lake Michigan's northern shore, from Iggy west to Menominee. This area traditionally gets a lot less snow than counties and geographic regions farther north, which means less snowpack, milder temps, and a longer growing season than areas farther north. [Author's note: Escanaba is often cited as the capital of the Yooper Banana Belt, but it seems to me that Menominee, being considerably farther south than Esky, ought to have that august designation.]

Yooper scooper = Used to push snow rather than lift it, as one does with a traditional snow shovel; much easier on the human back.

Yooper seasons, da four = Dere's winter, still-winter, almost-winter, and road construction ahead.

Yooper stooper = Can imply a hangover stupor, intoxication, or a combination thereof.

Yooper tennies = Hiking boots worn in summer (when not wearing swampers).

Yooper Trumpers = Rabid Yooper fans in Donald Trump's MAGA base.

yoosebiscuitness = ubiquitous

yoosta = used to, formerly

yote = Slang for coyote, though not in widespread use in the U.P.

you betcha = "Oh hell yes, I agree!" Oddly, Yoopers, who always say "youse," say "you" when they use the phrase "You betcha." [Author's note: It's a mystery.]

Youconned = Yukon; Limpy claims, "Da gold, she's all gone up dere, an' 'ere, eh?") [Author's note: Sorry, Limpy, but in this rare instance, you're incorrect. There was gold in the Ropes Gold Mine near Ishpeming, and soon there will be gold coming out of the Back Forty Mine in mid-Menominee County, where it shows up in concert with zinc ore.]

younk = an amateur; someone in over their head

Your Rope = Europe

youse = you (singular and plural), though sometimes you hear Limpy use "youse's" [Author's note: John McWhorter, associate professor of linguistics at Columbia University, has pointed out the relative peculiarity of the second-person "you" in English doing double duty as singular and plural, unlike in Elizabethan English, where and when there were more distinctions made for singular and plural, but also in distinctions of politeness. McWhorter points to the use of "youse" in the northern United States, calling it a "yeomanly" attempt to create a plural form of you by adding an "s." It may be that the good professor was unaware of our beloved Yoopers, but I would inform him at the outset that "youse" can be a dual-purpose singular and plural, if the speaker doesn't go fancy with the ponderously plural "youses." Further, I'd guess the whole youse "thing" came down to the Yoop from Canadian immigrants, and that Canadians no doubt took it down into Maine and the other northeastern states as well.]

Yousecrane = Ukraine; sayeth that great news hawk, Limpy: "Where da Russians trine taken over da place."

youseloggy = eulogy; "Nice words for da dead guy or girlie."

yowsome = attractive; good-looking

Yuckbuktu = "Any dose places where pipples eats puppy meat, monkey brains, squid guts, and/or snake bloods."

yuh = you, youse (singular and plural)

Yumpin' Yimminy = Faux Swedlingish for "Holy Cow!"

yut = yes

Z

za = pizza

zilcher = a loser; brings nothing to the table

zinc = sink

zing = "When youse mock youse's pals and chums, youse is 'zingin' 'em. Down sout' where Da Rebels live, dey call dis da red-assin'."

zizzies = sparks

zneeorty = frosty, freezing

zombullies = "Dose walkin' dead guys try push pipples aroun'."

zonktail = cocktail; "Youse 'ave too many dese an' youse's unner table pert quick."

zoosh = a tree stump

Part V

LIMPY'S FIFTEEN WAYS TA WRECKREATE IN DA YOOP

1. "Blast t'rough mud holes on da dirtbikes, snowmobiles, ATVs, Cheeps, dune buggies, etc."

2. "Fun dis way countin' da lightnin' bugs: Have shot a' beer after anybody calls out a lightnin' bug. Last one standin' wins what's left in da keck."

3. "When da white dirt comes down, try shackin', skitchin', hookin', etc.: Grab holt of the bumper of truck or car at stomp sign and let pull youse down a street, using youse's boot soles for da skis."

4. "Go huntin' an' fishin' wit' no license an' try fool da game wardens by not gettin' seen or pinched."

5. "Take da road-pops [beer] whenever an' wherever youse's gone ride, or drive. Never know when youse'll get da t'irsties."

6. "Road-hunt—shoot stuff from youse's truck—at night. Who gone find out?"

7. "Spear dose spawnin' steelhead an' walleyes. Dis is great fun in 'ippers or chess-waders."

8. "Snow-ski down dat Ashmun Hill in Da Soo. (Caution: Don't do dis in summer, even if youse's tippled a tad bit too many road-pops.)"

9. "Go out back, kick da bear's dat got 'is fat mush in youse's bird feeders."

10. "Call da game warden, tell 'im youse's neighbor's baitin' da deers or turkeys when baitin's illegal, or 'e's over limit."

11. "Call DNR tip line, give 'em names a every jamoke tryin' ta hunt near youse's blind an' proppity."

12. "Chase da wymyns at da bar. (But don't chase if 'er hubby dere wit' 'er.)"

13. "When wifeys an' girlies' hubbies, or da poyfriens, go huntin' camp, wifeys and wymyns go bar for da good times. Youse should mebbe go dere too for I t'ink da same reason."

14. "Drive roun' county, shoot da holes in traffic signs wit' da rifles an' scatterguns."

15. "Use da snowmobile ta jump over da open waters on frozed-up lakes."

Part VI

MEMORABLE QUOTES FROM POACHER VIOLATORS, AND ADMIRERS OF DA YOOP

Remark of astonishment from "hunter" in Delta County, standing in a tree, right beside a two-track, twenty feet up, decked out in full camo, face included, but wearing knee-high white swampers: **"Geez, Sir, howju see me up dere? I'm in da full-body camo, eh."** [Author's note: The officer, not wanting to crush the guy's ego completely with the obviously overlooked ignorance re: white boots, smiled benignly and said, "Camo doesn't make you invisible, dude."]

Iron Mountain turkey poacher: **"We onny tooken da ones dint fly off after we shot 'em."**

Response of a Pennsylvania hunter in the U.P. to the officer's request for his ID and hunting license, this hunter being in possession of drugs, and with a loaded gun in the vehicle at night: **"I got no ID. How 'bout my Splash card?"** [Author's note: This Splash card was the gent's seasonal pass to a water park somewhere in Pennsylvania. Predictably, said pass had expired.]

Question to officer from man accused of over-baiting for deer with excessive heads of cabbage: **"Does each leaf count, or jus' da heads?"** [Author's note: This gent has the mind of a constitutional originalist.]

Yooper hunter to CO who asked the man if his bait pile was two gallons, which was then the legal max: **"Uh, mebbe she'd be a little tad-bit over dat, eh?"** [Author's note: In actuality, the two-hundred-pound, eight-foot-long, waist-high pile was way beyond a little tad-bit over.]

One Yooper violator to his partner after his chum was pinched and the CO was citing the law and violation to the accused, who insisted he'd never heard of the law before: The partner lectured, **"Ignorance is no excusing da law."** [Author's note: Indeed. I think. The point of contention in this instance had been a law for *at least* twenty-five years.]

A Yooper had tagged a seven-point buck with his ninety-year-old father-in-law's license (the latter had Alzheimer's and was in a care center, and had not hunted in many years). The son-in-law had taken the old fellow to the store, where he bought a license for his daughter's hubby to use. After all was said and done, citations issued, etc., the bright bulb looked at the CO with a big grin and whined, **"Ya can't blame a guy for tryin'."** [Author's note: With a bow toward decency, I won't report here the CO's exact response, but I can assure you that it was a semi-profane collection of words that amounted to "Thank you for playing, asshole."]

How one poacher labeled the illegal elk in his freezer: **"Alks."** [Author's note: This fellow had been turned in by his ex-wife. He was found guilty and given a hefty fine, but it should be noted that the presiding judge did not sentence the man to remedial spelling or grammar class.]

This from a landowner who was livid that COs would come on his private property to fine him for baiting when baiting was outlawed: **"Youse were da enemies afore, but now youse are *really* da**

enemies." [Author's note: The bait pile was so large it had been spied by an aircraft passing over it. The deer paths in the snow were like spokes off a wheel hub.]

There was at one time a fellow in Crystal Falls, in Iron County, who collected roadkill, and in doing so helped keep eagles and other creatures from being killed or injured by vehicles. He collected the deer carcasses for meat, which he distributed to people. The side of his truck bore a great sign declaring **"UNDEERTAKER."** [Author's note: Initiative is initiative.]

Here is a remark from a gent who shot a deer that did not conform to the QDM (Quality Deer Management) regs on the number of points on one antler—and by the way, he also happened to shoot the animal from inside his vehicle at night, on a county highway: **"All I could see was they was horns, an' I got me a wifey an' four kids to feed."** [Author's note: A small technical observation at this juncture: As far as I know, horns are inedible, except perhaps to porcupines. Deer antlers are sold at steep prices in pet stores for dogs to gnaw on.] The hunter was convicted for an illegal deer, fined, and lost his hunting privileges for a number of years.

This is the seemingly genuinely befuddled response of a Wisconsin road hunter caught with a loaded rifle in his lap and his windows open, slow-rolling a county road in broad daylight. Here's what he said when the CO told him that such a hunting "technique" was illegal: **"Since *when*? I been comin' up here an' doin' this for *thirty years!*"** [Author's note: After sending the gent on his way, ticket in hand, my partner shuddered and remarked, "Thirty *years?* Kinda makes you wonder what the hell else we've been missing." He was a great game warden and partner. I would add, this kind of "road-hunting" is as illegal in Wisconsin as it is in Michigan. And has been for a long, long time.]

Most contacts where illegal activity is suspected occur in what one might call touchy circumstances, but seldom is there extreme violence. Verbal abuse is, of course, short of physical violence, but sometimes the emotions explode. This remark to the partner of the CO who was writing the man a ticket: **"You ogay, I like *you*—but your boss, *he* is a PRICK!"** [Author's note: The hunter was a Polish immigrant with a heavy accent, and he was arrested for possessing a light, and a loaded, uncased firearm in his vehicle the night before the deer season opener.]

Here's a standard response when COs ask if there's dope or alcohol in a vehicle they have just stopped: **"Not that I know of . . . but if there is, it ain't mine."** [Author's note: Translates to "Yes, it's here, but I want the other people with me to take the hit for it if I'm going to get tagged."]

There are many, many great admirers of the Yoop:
"It's an edgy place. I mean, in the sense that it still hangs on out there like a rawhide flap of the old frontier, outposted from the swirl of mainstream America. The U.P. is a hard place. A person has to want to hurt a lot to live there."

—John G. Mitchell, *Audubon* magazine, November 1981

"The best thing that could happen to the U.P. would be for someone to bomb the bridge."

—John D. Voelker, famous author, former Michigan Supreme Court justice, from Ishpeming

"That land of wonderful wilderness."

—Edwin Way Teale, *Journey into Summer*, 1960

"As a child living in the northern part of the Lower Peninsula, I felt cheated with a winter of light snow. Lights snowfalls rarely happen in the Upper Peninsula, which can get 300 inches a year along Superior, a preposterous amount. I loved visiting in winter, though I couldn't reach my cabin because of the deep snow. These people have learned over the centuries how to deal with the vast accumulations of snow. I was never truly inconvenienced.

"There is also a tradition in the Upper Peninsula that you never pass by anyone needing help. An Ojibwa Indian once towed me 60 miles after I broke a fan belt on Fourth of July weekend. He seemed startled that I couldn't install a fan belt. A gas station had a spare, which he installed. He wouldn't accept money, so I stuffed a C note in his wife's pocket. She smiled, having more sense than he did. Where can you find someone to tow you 60 miles and install your fan belt? Only in the U.P."

—Jim Harrison, "Jim Harrison's Upper Peninsula,"
New York Times, December 1, 2013

Part VII

GAME WARDENSPEAK

area = There are presently twelve DNR law enforcement districts in Michigan, each district divided into areas, each area containing several counties. A sergeant is responsible for an area; a lieutenant is responsible for the district; and there are three captains: one for the U.P. and Upper Michigan; a second for Lower Michigan; and the third captain is assigned to HQ in Lansing with the chief of DNR law enforcement.

AVL = Automatic Vehicle Locator; a system that allows Lansing to see all officers at all times anywhere in the state. This system is not in use much anymore, having been replaced by more advanced electronics and technology.

backup = This is where one officer is either in position to come to the support of another, or racing forward to help another officer who has signaled for assistance. All police officers, whatever their agency, respond to backup calls from other officers, whether from their own or other agencies, *subito.*

bad guy = lawbreaker, violator

bait = Food used by hunters to attract game animals; then, those bait-attracted animals themselves become bait for officers monitoring illegal hunting.

barrel trap = Used to capture troublesome black bears. Although bru-
ins captured thusly are moved far away from the point of capture
before being released, black bears have an uncanny sense of place,
and often find their way back.

bikini float = Basically, a floating drunk-roundup on a river or lake
in summertime when rivers are crammed with commercial canoes
and rafts, etc.

binos = binoculars

biscuit = a ticket

blue light = emergency lights on CO law enforcement trucks

boots in the dirt, snow, etc. = COs spend a lot of time in their patrol trucks, but even more time walking, observing, and checking
sportsmen. Officers are out in all kinds of weather, every day of the
week; even if one officer has the day off, others will cover.

bubbles and sticks = signals of connectivity on smart (and other) cell
phones and various devices

bump = to call on the telephone or other electronic device

bush vision = Someone with this trait has keen eyesight, and is able
to see *everything* when they are in the woods.

chipmunking = excessive (unecessary) chatter on police radios

clanlab = clandestine drug lab; these days, largely methamphetamine ops

clear = A radio term that means "My radio transmission is finished."

clear of the last = "I've safely departed the last situation I reported
going into." All officers report locations, vehicle descriptions, and
so forth, *before* making contact with the public.

closed season = Those locations, dates, and times of year when and where certain fish or game cannot be legally taken.

CO = conservation officer

come-along = A hand-operated strap used to extract disabled vehicles from various troubles.

condemnation hearings = Court proceedings where judge rules on requests by prosecutors to condemn and destroy guns and other equipment used in the commission of various crimes.

creep = to stealthily approach (sneak up on) something from a place of concealment

crew = a group of violators working together

crow / crow line = Citizens in league with lawbreakers, and often themselves anti-DNR, who act as lookouts to signal violators whenever they see DNR law enforcement trucks in an area. A crow line is a series of these lookouts.

cub = An older term for an officer in field training, fresh out of many months of rigorous DNR Academy training. Nowadays this officer is more likely to be called a PCO (probationary conservation officer).

dead month = Jargon for the month of March, usually the public's lowest ebb in outdoor activities during the year, and thus a dead month for game wardens.

deer guard = A steel contraption welded to patrol truck grills to help limit damage from collisions with deer.

Dep = slang for any county sheriff's deputy

dimed out = informed on; tipped off

dirtball / wingnut / frequent flyer = Three of many terms used by officers to refer to repeat violators.

DNR or MDNR = Department of Natural Resources or Michigan Department of Natural Resources

DNR Academy = All CO trainees must graduate from this program based near Lansing, the full version of which lasts nine months. Only four to five of the approximately five thousand people in the state civil service candidate pool (at any given time) will ever qualify for a DNR Academy class. The class size averages about twenty to twenty-five candidates, out of which fifteen to twenty will graduate and get through their full PCO (probationary conservation officer) year.

DNR priors = The Fish and Game rap sheets for previous violations are computerized and available to officers on demand, and are also used for data on current and past outdoor licenses.

doubleback = This is a term for when officers check a camp or location, find violations, discuss them with the citizens involved, take appropriate action, including directing them to clean it up—and then come back another time to ensure that the cleanup or corrective action has been taken.

drag trail = Indications that a game animal has been pulled out of the woods, usually to a vehicle.

Drive School = A special, highly demanding, offensive and defensive vehicle operator's training that all officers must undergo and be able to pass on a regular basis.

drop-off = This is a practice whereby violators drop off one crew member to either illegally shoot an animal or to locate one they've previously shot. The vehicle drops off the individual and then leaves the area, returning later to recover the individual and the "prize." Often they are also met by a CO truck or two.

EGLE = Department of Environment, Great Lakes, and Energy. This is the independent department that houses environmental conservation officers (ECOs).

eighty-twenty = The belief that 80 percent of hunters are legit and capable, while 20 percent remain slobs and/or incompetent.

exotic = any imported wildlife

exposure suit = Worn by COs and other law enforcement personnel on lakes and other water bodies during winter and other cold or extreme conditions. These high-tech suits provide warmth if an officer accidentally goes overboard while on patrol.

eyes-in-the-sky = Aircraft or drones used to support law enforcement ground operations; a very simple but sophisticated law enforcement strategy, the tactics and skills for which were developed some decades back by Michigan pilot-COs.

fair chase = A marketing/sales claim made by some hunting ranches and other trophy operations to let potential well-heeled customers know that their kill-for-cash offerings are "fair." The definition of "fair chase" varies by establishment.

Feeb = slang for FBI special agent, or someone who is feebleminded

fire officer = DNR personnel in district offices charged with monitoring fire conditions and leading/coordinating firefighting efforts when seasonal fires crop up.

first on scene = The responding officer who is first to arrive on the scene of an accident, crime, or incident, and usually becomes responsible for managing the incident.

fish biologist lingo/terms = *anadramous*: fish which live in salt water and migrate to freshwater rivers to spawn (e.g., salmon, some brown trout, some brook trout); *adfluvial*: fish which live in large freshwater bodies such as the Great Lakes and migrate up rivers to spawn (e.g., salmon, brown trout, steelhead, brook trout [coasters]); *semelparity*: those species that spawn once and die (e.g., most salmon); *iteroparity*: those species that spawn multiple times during their lifetimes (e.g., humans). (Personally, iteroparity sounds like a lot more fun than the alternative.)

flee, or elude = Fancy words for suspects who try to run and hide from officers; almost none succeed.

flipping = Seeing something that requires an officer's immediate attention leads him to make a quick 180-degree turnaround to catch up with the other vehicle and address the situation.

floater = A drowned body that is either driven to the surface by the buildup of internal gases, or the body has been released by anchor ice where it had been hung up.

float-your-hat = To lose your footing while wading a river and to be swept downstream. Usually your hat travels farther and faster than you do.

flying fish = Violators in boats sometimes throw their catch over the gunwales while being pursued by COs.

free forty = This is officer jargon for unpaid time, most often in connection with firearms deer season, which is the busiest time for officers in most parts of the state.

FTO (field training officer) = Experienced officers assigned to work with, train, coach, mentor, and evaluate new PCOs during three several-month-long field-training periods following successful completion of the formal DNR Academy program.

furlough = Unpaid days off for officers, a management method for controlling departmental expense and the state budget, especially in periods where public money is short.

game wardens = An old term for conservation officers, though still often in common use, especially in rural areas of the state, including the U.P.

Garden "Wars" = A term for the violent conflict that took place from the 1960s through the 1980s on the Garden Peninsula in the Upper Peninsula, when local commercial fishermen operated illegally and in open violation of commercial fishing regulations.

ginseng = A plant, native to the entire state, used in Eastern medicine; it can be found all around the state, and there are now some commercial growers, both ATB and BTB. It is legal to harvest along lakeshores with a DNR permit.

goat rodeo = Slang for any operation that goes awry. In the military this term is known as FUBAR (Fucked Up Beyond All Recognition) or SNAFU (Situation Normal: All Fouled Up).

gork = a term for badly mutilated human remains

Got a question for you . . . = The most common opening line or greeting of citizens to conservation officers.

ground shrinkage = A hunter shoots a game animal, usually a bear, from an elevated platform or tree stand, and after climbing down and locating the animal, finds it is smaller than judged from the perch above. Ooh boy.

group patrol = When multiple COs come together to focus concentrated manpower on certain activities in specific areas at designated times. It's sometimes called "flooding an area with badges."

GSW = gunshot wound

headlighting = Sweeping your headlights across fields where deer may be grazing.

head-on stop = A maneuver to stop a suspect vehicle coming directly toward the officer; a tense and *very* dangerous situation.

Henry Hill = Grady Service term for "headless and hide," the usual leave-behinds of deer violators.

Horseblankets = Old-time game wardens wore shapeless, massive wool coats, like the greatcoats worn in World War I. Younger officers at one time referred to these older COs as "Horseblankets," a term of honor and great respect.

illegal deer = An animal taken out of season; or in season by illegal means; or in a restricted area closed to hunting by the state (for various reasons); or by someone unlicensed to take a deer, or who failed to tag an animal.

in-and-out = Tire tracks showing a vehicle has gone into and back out of a location. All COs are taught how to interpret/read tire-tread tracks, and how to backtrack them.

informant = What in popular culture is sometimes called a "narc"; it refers to a citizen who provides information to conservation officers about possible illegal activity. Informant identities are protected, and they are given anonymity. In some instances, informants receive monetary awards from the state.

jacklighting = *see* "shining"

lamping = Term from Britain and Europe for using lights at night to legally hunt foxes. This practice is illegal in Michigan.

LED = law enforcement division

LHA = The lost hunter alert is a procedure for setting up and co-ordinating law enforcement agencies and others to search for a lost hunter.

light them up = To turn on the truck's emergency blue lights as a signal to subjects that they should *immediately* pull over to the side of the road and stop.

marble eyes = The eyes of dead deer undergo certain known and charted changes, which allows officers to quickly identify when an animal was killed.

marine duty = COs not only patrol on land but also on state waters, in boats, kayaks, jet skis, canoes, etc.

market hunters = Violators who kill fish and game for commercial meat markets, primarily in Midwestern urban centers.

marking a deer = Method of marking illegally downed animals and later confronting violators with evidence of the animals' provenance.

marking a road = COs are taught multiple methods for marking roads to allow them to quickly determine if there has been any recent use.

meat hunter = Someone who hunts for food, not trophies.

Miracle Hour = That hour just before sunset and sunrise when animals tend to be moving from bedding locations to feeding areas. A prime time for hunters, which COs do not disturb unless they have information (a complaint or allegation) that a violation is under way.

mortality signal = DNR biologists capture and tag various wild creatures with radio collars in order to study species movement. When animals die, their transmitters, triggered by lack of movement within a certain amount of time, transmit a particular solid-tone signal. Handheld antennae are then employed to locate the animal on the ground.

necropsy = An animal autopsy to determine cause and time of death (if relevant), or changes wrought by disease.

night-shoot = All Michigan law enforcement agencies must be proficient in firearms use under all kinds of conditions. COs participate in night-shooting training sessions.

nose- or face-plant = To fall on your face, or to put a suspect on the ground on their face for resisting or failure to comply. Suspects taken to the ground are immediately handcuffed and gotten back to their feet.

NVD = Night vision device; COs have a wide range of the most modern night-vision technology.

officer caution = An advisory to officers to be careful, or requiring multiple officers when dealing with certain individuals, even on semi-routine matters.

Oh-dark thirty = This jargon describes working deep into the night. Night is when illegal activity often occurs and the bad guys in some places are most active, and night is when the work of a CO is at its most dangerous. [Author's note: This term jogs my memory of Shakespeare and a conservation officer's reality, the line from Sonnet 97, "What freeezings have I felt, what dark days seen!" There was for a time a story about Shakespeare, alleging that he had been caught poaching deer, and had run off to London to escape prosecution. No evidence has ever surfaced to confirm this, but the depth and breadth of knowledge of nature we see in Will's work seems to suggest he had more than a passing interest in the outdoors.

You probably never expected to encounter Shakespeare in a book about Limpy Allerdyce's colorfully convoluted language, but here it is—and it's not simply this author's sappy indulgence. Many of the words and phrases invented and/or coined by the great William Shakespeare in the late sixteenth and early seventeenth centuries are still in use in common English today, even in Da Yoop (set in italics in following examples): Because night police work is so dangerous, COs have to be made of *sterner stuff* and always at the top of their games, so as not to be led on *wild goose chases* when *something wicked their way comes*. Our officers are trained to use the night as their tool against violators, so that when the sun rises, and *what's done is done*, they can't *melt into the air*. As Shakespeare's Banquo once warned Macbeth, ". . . the instruments of darkness tell us truths, only to betray us in the end." COs who are trained and equipped to use darkness against bad guys don't get betrayed in the end, as did the players in *Macbeth*. Writer as poacher? Not such an outrageous concept. Ernest Hemingway got busted by a Michigan game warden at his folks' place on Walloon Lake—but that's a story for another time.]

"Out of service" = Phrase used by officer to call Lansing and/or local Dispatch, when going off shift. It means, "I'm done for the day or night."

"Out of vehicle" = Alert to local Dispatch, and/or Lansing, that the officer is getting out of the patrol truck at a particular location or address. When the officer finishes and gets back into the truck, the officer calls "Clear of the last" to let everyone know the situation is copasetic.

parroting = When subjects begin to repeat the questions they are being asked, it can be a sign of stress, and the fact that they may have something to hide or are trying to buy time to think by repeating the questions before answering them. Officers are trained in interview techniques and quickly pick up on body language and other clues, such as this one.

pass day(s) = a CO's day(s) off

PBT = preliminary breath test; used in the field to help determine sobriety

PCO = probationary conservation officer

POO = point of origin; exact location where a fire originates

pop-out = An officer suddenly materializes out of nowhere, and the surprised civilians respond excitedly, "Where the hell did *you* come from?"

printable offense = Any offense that calls for individuals to be fingerprinted when they are arrested and brought into custody.

Quiet Time = Predetermined number of days before the opening of firearms deer season when no guns may be possessed in the field. Guns may be transported to camp, but then must remain there. This term also applies to rules that forbid the operation of ATVs during certain hours of the days during hunting season.

rake = Nickname for any officer whose thorough and aggressive patrolling has kept down lawlessness in his or her area of responsibility.

RAM Center = The Ralph A. McMullen Center, named for a former DNR director. Once a Civilian Conservation Corps (CCC) site, it's now a DNR and state meeting facility on North Higgins Lake, about two hours' drive BTB.

RAP Line = Report All Poaching, a 1-800 telephone line for the public, manned 24/7 in Lansing. Calls and complaints from the public are passed immediately to officers in the field to address as needed. All calls are held in strict confidence.

recon shuffle = A fast, steady shuffling trot used by some COs to cover a lot of ground on foot, day and night.

recruit = a member of the current DNR Academy class

regular customer = repeat offender

ride-along = Under certain circumstances and following specific procedures, civilians may be allowed to ride with COs on their daily patrols. There are, of course, multiple forms to be filled out, and permissions to be secured.

Roadie = Jargon for "Retired on Active Duty," referring to an officer who for whatever reason has lost enthusiasm for the job. A *very* rare occurrence, but it does happen.

roadkill = animals schmucked along the state's roadways

rolling (mobile) lab = Illegal methamphetamine lab set up in a vehicle and operated on remote rural roads. This sort of thing is a severe public safety hazard.

Roof, The = Slang for Marquette DNR Regional Service Office, which features a unique architectural design.

RSS = Retail sales system; Lansing has complete license-purchase histories on all hunters and anglers, etc., available to officers in the field, during contacts with subjects.

rubber gun school = remedial firearms training

runner = An individual who flees and eludes an encounter with an officer, either before contact, or after it has begun. A very poor life choice.

schmuck = Onomatopoeic term for killing or striking something or someone with a vehicle. (*Onomatopoeic* means a word that phonetically resembles or suggests the sound it describes, e.g., "bang" or "coo.")

Secret Squirrel = Slang for DNR detectives; their biz cards say they're detectives, so I'm not sure what's secret about it. Detectives support field officers with advanced investigatory skills and support, and especially with assistance when writing complex search warrants, etc.

secure = Periodic officer report to Dispatch to confirm he or she is safe and the situation is under control.

sharking = Term for an officer who cruises close to where another officer is in the process of confronting subjects. The shark is in position to bring quick backup to the situation, if needed.

shining = Using artificial light to temporarily freeze deer in their tracks at night and shoot them. Also called jacklighting and headlighting (the latter using car headlights rather than another artificial light to illuminate the deer).

shit magnet = A term of admiration for officers who have a knack for seeking out and intervening in all kinds of wrongdoing. It's not an acquired skill so much as an innate condition for some officers. Fictional character Grady Service is a prime example of a shit magnet. Rakes are often *extreme* shit magnets.

sitting on a camp = Surveillance of a place which may or may not be a camp, but where there is evidence, and often have been reports, of questionable activities. Surveillance may be done day or night.

skins = patrol truck tires

slow-roller = A vehicle moving very slowly on a two-track or county road, day or night. Slow speed can be a signal of illegal hunting in process (or a drunk driver).

Station 20 = Lansing DNR Law Enforcement Headquarters

step-out = Term for dismounting a moving patrol vehicle. This was a common term many decades ago, although the technique is no longer taught, or encouraged. A highly risky move at best.

stroke = to write or issue a ticket or citation

subject = Jargon for an individual an officer is dealing with, who is not necessarily a suspect.

swoop team = When a couple of officers surveil a situation, and others stand by to swoop onto the scene.

tag = State-issued record each hunter must affix to a deer immediately after killing it, even *before* gutting the deer. The tag requires the successful hunter to notch the tag to indicate what he has killed, and when. (It says right on the tag to affix it immediately.)

take a little walk = CO talk for leaving one's truck or ATV and proceeding on foot for a "walk" that can last fifteen minutes, five miles, or ten hours. When an officer says, "Let's take a little walk," you have no idea what lies ahead.

TOD = time of death

Torpedo = A small lead device with treble hooks that looks like a lure but is primarily an illegal fish-snagging instrument. It is dragged and jerked along like a small grappling hook. The Torpedo developed after the outlawing of Silver Spiders, which are one- to two-ounce chunks of lead soldered onto treble hooks and used the same way Torpedos are used, but lacking the attempted visual misrepresentation of a legit lure.

Tribal game warden = An individual employed by Michigan's Native American Tribal governments. The Tribal officers often work with and back up Michigan COs, and Michigan COs back up Tribal wardens as well.

Troop = slang for a Michigan State Police (MSP) officer

unmarked = an unmarked state-owned vehicle

TX = telephone

VCO = A voluntary conservation officer, a now-defunct DNR law enforcement program wherein certain qualified civilians were given formal training and became regular partners or full-time COs. Other states still employ VCOs.

wants and warrants = Each time a CO is about to contact a subject in the computer, records are checked to make sure the individual has no outstanding wants or warrants.

weed patch = illegal marijuana field

wrestling = Term used by COs to refer to any physical confrontation with suspects.